THE CAPTIVES

Emma Leslie Church History Series

Glaucia the Greek Slave
A Tale of Athens in the First Century

The Captives
Or, Escape from the Druid Council

Out of the Mouth of the Lion
Or, The Church in the Catacombs

Sowing Beside All Waters
A Tale of the World in the Church

From Bondage to Freedom
A Tale of the Times of Mohammed

The Martyr's Victory
A Story of Danish England

Gytha's Message
A Tale of Saxon England

GUNTRA GOING TO MEET THE
DRUID COUNCIL   PAGE 21

EMMA LESLIE CHURCH HISTORY SERIES

THE CAPTIVES

OR, ESCAPE FROM THE DRUID COUNCIL

BY

EMMA LESLIE

"The dark places of the earth are full of the
habitations of cruelty..."
Psalm 74:20

SALEM RIDGE PRESS
EMMAUS, PENNSYLVANIA

Originally Published
1873
Sunday School Union

Republished 2007
Salem Ridge Press LLC
4263 Salem Drive
Emmaus, Pennsylvania 18049

www.salemridgepress.com

Hardcover ISBN: 978-1-934671-02-3
Softcover   ISBN: 978-1-934671-03-0

PUBLISHER'S NOTE

In *The Captives* Emma Leslie uses the love of a mother for her children and the love of a brother for his little sister to picture for us, and them, the amazing love of God. As we seek to impact the world around us we can take comfort in the fact that God reached out to each of us while we were still in rebellion: "But God commendeth his love toward us, in that, while we were yet sinners, Christ died for us" (Romans 5:8). God's love, demonstrated by Jesus Christ, is still changing lives today!

Daniel Mills

October, 2007

HISTORICAL NOTES

In 55 B.C. Julius Cæsar led the first Roman invasion of the island of Britain. He did very little conquering but convinced many of the tribes to pay tribute to him in exchange for peace. Over the next several decades, Rome supported the local kings and queens as they ruled their own fiercely independent tribes. Although several invasions were planned, a full-scale Roman invasion of Britain did not come until almost one hundred years later.

In A.D. 43, Roman forces led by General Aulus Plautius conquered southern Britain. Soon after this, the Roman city of Londinium (London) was established, and magnificent temples were built to Diana and Apollo. Then, in A.D. 60, six years before *The Captives* takes place, British Queen Boudica rebelled against the Romans. She attacked and destroyed several cities, culminating in the burning of Londinium and the brutal killing of thousands of Romans who were too old or weak to escape. The Roman army retaliated and in a decisive battle, killed tens of thousands of Boudica's warriors. Boudica herself then committed suicide.

Over the next few centuries, the Romans continued to expand their territory but their efforts

HISTORICAL NOTES

were often hampered by Britain's distance from
Rome and political unrest throughout the Em-
pire. By the fifth century the weakened Roman
Empire was no longer able to maintain control
of Britain, opening the way for invasion by the
Saxon peoples from northern Germany.

Two of the minor characters in *The Captives* are
based on a quote from Paul in his second letter to
Timothy which reads:

*Do thy diligence to come before winter. Eubulus
greeteth thee, and **Pudens**, and Linus, and **Claudia**,
and all the brethren.*

II Timothy 4:21

Scholars, including Archbishop James Usshur,
author of *The Annals of the World* in the 17th century, have associated the Claudia listed in *II Timothy* with Claudia Rufina, a British princess in the
first century who was the wife of Roman centurion Aulus Pudens. It is not known for sure if this
is the case.

IMPORTANT DATES

B.C.

55 Julius Cæsar invades Britain

54 Julius Cæsar's second invasion of Britain

A.D.

30 Jesus Christ crucified

43 General Aulus Plautius invades Britian

50 The City of Londinium is founded

54 Nero becomes Emperor of Rome

60 British Queen Boudica and her tribe
     burn Londinium

68 The Apostle Paul put to death

CONTENTS

ILLUSTRATIONS

THE CAPTIVES

THE ROMAN SOLDIER

THE CAPTIVES

CHAPTER I

THE MEETING IN THE WOODS

IT was a sweet peaceful scene that the midday sun looked down upon, as it glanced between the branches of the fine old oak trees, and penciled lines of golden light on the soft green grass and waving ferns that grew nowhere so luxuriantly as in the forests of Britain. Even the proud Roman could not but feel his heart touched with the sweetness of nature here, so different from the luxuries of art to which he was accustomed in his home on the banks of the Tiber; and it seemed that even a soldier could appreciate the sweetness and quietness of the forest glade; for presently the ferns were crushed into the grass by the foot of a middle-aged man dressed in the imperial uniform.

Throwing himself on the grass, the soldier heaved a sigh as he looked up towards the deep blue of the summer sky above, and uttered slowly, "The dark places of the earth are full of the habitations of cruelty;"[1] the old Jew was right in this. He shuddered at the recollection of a hideous scene he had witnessed in this fair land of Britain he had come to conquer, but found so hard to subdue. No wonder that the people, though simple in their manner of life, were fierce and cruel, when their priests and lawgivers, the Druids, practiced such wholesale murder in the performance of their religious rites; and once more the man shuddered, soldier though he was, at the mental picture that rose before him again—the hideous wicker image filled with men, women, and children, being set on fire by a white-robed priest, who at the same time carefully guarded the sacred spray of mistletoe he had just cut with a silver knife from a neighbouring oak, while, amid the shrieks and groans of the victims, the flames and smoke went curling up towards heaven, until the awful silence of death settled down upon the scene, broken only by the chanting of the priests as they performed their mysterious rites.

While still thinking of this, a slight noise attracted the soldier's attention, and looking round he saw an aged, venerable-looking man, in the garb of a Druid, standing at the entrance of a small cave hollowed out of a sandbank close by; but the next minute the sounds of a hunt were heard, and the soldier had only time to spring to his feet, when

---

[1] PSALM 74:20

VENERABLE: *commanding respect, impressive*

a huge boar, its bristles all erect with fury, came tearing down one of the forest alleys, and the next moment would have been upon him had he not hastily stepped aside and given him room to pass.

The dogs were not far behind, and the huge beast being well-nigh spent with his long run, was caught a few paces beyond; and before he could escape his tormenting little captors, a bold, handsome-looking youth came up and finished him with his broad hunting-knife.

The Roman soldier looked at the young Briton, for he knew he was a Briton, and not one of the trading Gauls who had settled on the coast, by the long fair hair that fell almost to his waist, as well as the stalwart limbs and proud defiant carriage, and he wondered whether he would ever be taken and offered as a peace offering to the cruel deity he worshiped, or whether those sturdy limbs would wield spear and battle-axe against the all-conquering eagles of Rome.

The young Briton needed no assistance in dispatching the boar when once he had brought him to bay, and did not seem to know that anyone was near, until turning to bind up the wounds of one of his dogs, he noticed the Druid standing at the entrance of the cave. He at once left the dog, and stepping respectfully forward, bowed before the priest.

"Thou art the son of Guntra, art thou not?" said the Druid as he drew near.

GAULS: *the inhabitants of western Europe*
STALWART: *strong*
CARRIAGE: *way of carrying himself*

With a low obeisance the Briton answered, "I am, most reverend teacher."

"And thou art anxious, I hear, to rid thy country of these foreign marmots, the Romans. Is it so?"

"Yes," answered the Briton, his blue eyes flashing angrily, and his hand instinctively grasping his powerful hunting-knife more firmly as he spoke.

The Druid saw the action. "And thou art ready to risk liberty and life for the sake of thy country, this fair but enslaved Britain, and to preserve the religion of thy forefathers from the violation of strangers?" said the Druid.

"I will not only risk my life, but give it," said the Briton, firmly; "I hate the Roman eagle, and will ever wage war against it and all it brings from Rome."

"That is well-said, my son," remarked the Druid, complacently; "it may be that the gods of these our free forests will demand your life, but you will but pass to another stage of existence, perchance to be a bird warbling amid our giant oaks, or a noble warhorse, that inspired by thy spirit shall perform deeds of prowess that shall make the Roman eagles quail in terror at his approach."

The Roman soldier from the shelter of the fern covert heard every word, and decided to report it to the centurion when he reached the neighbouring camp of London, for he was journeying from the distant camp of York, where he had been stationed since his return from Syria. He

OBEISANCE: *bow*
MARMOTS: *groundhogs; used as an insult*
PROWESS: *exceptional bravery or skill*

did not care to be seen just now by either the
Briton or the Druid, and yet he felt scarcely equal
to resuming his journey at once, and another
thing, he did not wish to miss his companions,
who were likewise resting in the forest, and whom
he had left, that he might read from a small roll
of parchment he carried beneath his breastplate,
and which had been given to him before he left
Cæsarea.

So he lay still among the tall sheltering ferns,
and drew out the parchment from its hiding-place,
and slowly read the words that told of eternal life
being gained for all by the voluntary death of the
man Christ Jesus. Reading was an art he had only
lately acquired, and so he could not do more than
spell out a few words, but those few told of life
and immortality beyond the grave. Very different
teaching from what he had learned about his family Penates in his old Roman home, and very different from the reward held forth by the Druid to
the young Briton just now.

Marcinius was thinking of this, and slowly rolling up his parchment again, when the ferns by
which he was surrounded were hastily pushed
aside, and the young Briton stood before him.

"How darest thou to venture within the sacred
precincts of this forest?" he demanded.

The soldier sprang to his feet, and instinctively
grasped the javelin at his side. But the next moment he had dropped it, for the young Briton was

COVERT: *covering or hiding-place*
PENATES: *general household gods*
PRECINCTS: *a clearly defined area*

unarmed; he had left his hunting-knife in the boar which he killed.

"Dost thou ask that of a Roman?" said Marcinius, folding his arms across defiantly.

"Yes, I, a free-born Briton, ask thee, Roman dog, how thou darest to provoke the wrath of our forest spirits by venturing under the shadow of these sacred oaks?"

"By the right of conquest," Marcinius was about to reply; but he checked these words, and said more gently, "I came here to rest awhile and read certain parchments for my soul's refreshment;" and as he spoke he held forth the roll in proof of his assertion.

The Briton stepped back a pace or two in dumb surprise, as if fearing the roll of parchment should touch him, as in truth he was, much more so than of the flashing sharp-pointed javelin; for the fact of any but a Druid being able to read, was in itself so startling that he was half-afraid one of the dreaded forest spirits had taken the form of a Roman soldier, to wreak vengeance upon him for some unknown insult.

But after gazing a minute or two in silent wonder at Marcinius, the young Briton began to feel reassured that it was no phantom before him, and he ventured to say, "Do thy gods allow thee to pry into their mysteries by means of that?" and he pointed to the roll half-fearfully as he spoke.

"This is a message from my God," said Marcinius, reverently.

A look of contempt stole over the young Briton's face. "Your gods who dwell in temples such as that, standing in the center of yonder camp at London, must indeed be poor and pitiful to send a message to such as you," he said, in a tone of disdain.

A haughty smile curled the lips of the Roman for a minute, but he answered quietly, "I worship not your adopted goddess, Diana, whose temple is in our camp or Apollo, whose temple is just beyond, but my God is the Lord who dwells in heaven, and not in temples made with hands."

"You worship our forest spirits then, for they disdain anything but unhewn granite and the free air of heaven; they cannot be confined in any temple," said the young Briton, quickly.

But the Roman shook his head: "I worship the God of the whole earth; but He is not cruel like your forest spirits, He is the God of love and kindness."

"Love and kindness!" repeated the Briton, and he burst into a mocking laugh. "Commend me to your God when I need love and kindness," he said, and turned on his heel and walked back to his dogs and his employment of cutting off the head of the boar. The same mocking smile crossed his lips again and again as he went on with his work; and he again repeated the words "love and kindness" as he looked towards the fern covert where he had left the Roman soldier. He was not there now, he could see, or he might have stepped across to ask something else about this despised God, for what could be more despicable than a God of love? thought the fierce young Briton as he strode homewards, swinging the boar's head by one ear, and closely followed by his dogs.

A God of love! why he, Jugurtha, the son of Guntra, was half-ashamed of the love he bore his mother and little sister, and hoped to conquer it by and by, though he had come out to hunt the boar this morning purposely for his mother, that she might have her favourite dish of boar's head for supper.

When he got beyond the forest he came out upon a wide plain, dotted with short-horned red cattle and flocks of sheep. In the center of this plain stood several mysterious-looking piles of stones, and close by a charred blackened space, looking like a huge blot on the fair landscape.

Fierce though he was, the young Briton turned his eyes from that place of sacrifice. He almost despised himself for doing it, and looked forward to the time when he, like the Druids themselves, and all the older men of his tribe, should be able to look complacently on such sacrifices as were offered there; but now it brought a sickening horror, and he hurried past it on to the little village of huts beyond.

It was the poorest attempt at building one could well-imagine, this village of the proud Britons. They despised their lordly conquerors, the Romans, for their love of luxury and refinement, and certainly there was no approach here to either the one or the other. A group of huts built of the branches of trees, interlaced and covered with sods of turf set down without any attempt at order, was all they could boast of in the way of architecture, and the internal arrangements were equally simple. A heap of wolfskins, that could be used as mats to sit upon by day, formed with a heap of dried leaves their beds at night. In their dress there was very little difference between that of the men and women; a rough sheepskin garment covered their bodies, while arms and legs were painted blue. There was, however, one notable exception in this particular. A tall, handsome, imperious-looking woman stood in the doorway of the largest of the huts, dressed in a long white flowing robe, and a little girl playing at her side likewise wore a loose-fitting garment of white wool.

The woman was looking earnestly and anxiously towards the plain where the cattle grazed, but as she caught sight of Jugurtha striding along with his dogs, the look of anxiety left her face, and she heaved a sigh of relief. "Once more I shall see him," she murmured; "once more will his noble head rest beneath this roof before—" and she

IMPERIOUS: *commanding, noble*

turned aside her head, for the child at her side was looking up in her face wonderingly.

"Jugurtha is coming," she said, stooping to kiss the little girl's upturned face. "He has killed the boar, I can see," she added, as she shaded her eyes, and once more looked towards the plain.

"Is he bringing home the head?" asked the child, with an exclamation of delight.

"Yes, my little Norma, I can see it in his hand," said her mother, scarcely less delighted than the child. She valued it, not for the savoury dish the boar's head would make, but because it was flavoured with a son's love.

A few minutes afterwards, Jugurtha had reached the hut, and thrown the still bleeding head at his mother's feet, yet so carefully that not a spot stained her long robe. Little but imperiousness was seen in the mother's face, for she was the head of this tribe who dwelt in the village, and owned the sheep and cattle in the plain and some of the men were gathering round her now, bringing complaints of more cattle being stolen by the Romans.

Jugurtha heard the complaints, and then flourishing his hunting-knife above his head, he exclaimed, "I will go forth and rid the land of these oppressors; our forest spirits will help me, for they too have been insulted, their sacred groves have been invaded by the enemy, and now they shall be swept from our shores."

A loud shout was raised at the close of the young man's speech, for every Briton was united in this hatred of the Romans; but as it died away a look of anxiety, rather than of triumph, stole over the faces of the older men. They had fought against the Romans, and knew that undisciplined bravery; though ever so heroic, was no match for the trained veterans who fought beneath the all-conquering eagles of Rome; and they gazed at Jugurtha with a look of pity as they thought of the bitter disappointment that was in store for him.

But Jugurtha did not notice these looks. "My mother," he said, "will you not command me to take spear and target, and go forth against the oppressors of our people?"

The mother's bosom heaved for a moment with exultant pride as she gazed at her noble son, but she said slowly, "We must not act hastily or unadvisedly in this matter, we must wait until the council of Druids has met, and abide by their decision;" and as she spoke a spasm of agony crossed her face.

Jugurtha looked surprised. He had thought that the ceremony of investiture had merely been delayed on account of his youth—that his mother had chosen him long since to be one of her warriors, for he had often heard her say *he* was to save his tribe from the Roman power; and now he was anxious to do this, it seemed the matter was uncertain.

TARGET: *a small shield*
INVESTITURE: *commissioning*

He was inclined to feel impatient, until he heard that a council of all the principal Druids in the neighbourhood was to be held the following day, and that his mother had been summoned to attend it. "I will go with you, my mother, and plead with the wise men to be allowed to join our band of warriors at once," said Jugurtha, quickly.

But the lady shook her head decisively, while the same look of pain stole into her face again.

"Nay, nay, my son, that cannot be," she said; "I will bear your wishes to the council, and plead for you, too."

How earnest that pleading would be, Jugurtha did not know, or its object either. The deep anxiety that seemed to have settled upon his mother for the rest of the day he thought was caused by the loss of the cattle. He little knew how every movement was watched by those eager hungry eyes, as though they might be the last she would ever see.

CHAPTER II

THE SACRED COUNCIL

THE council of Druids had been sitting some hours in deliberation before Guntra, the mother of Jugurtha, reached the spot. The white-robed venerable-looking lawgivers were seated in a semicircle under the spreading branches of an old oak, and within sight of the grey moss-grown stones that witnessed their mysterious rites of worship.

A dead silence prevailed as Guntra drew near. A dozen of the oldest men of her tribe had accompanied her to within a short distance of the spot, and now waited until the conference should be over. The lady made a low obeisance when within a few steps of the circle, for though the chief of a tribe, every outward respect was demanded by the all-powerful Druids, and Guntra was especially anxious to conciliate them today.

"Guntra, daughter of Britain, what hast thou to say?" asked one, as the lady raised her head.

"It is of my son Jugurtha I would speak," said the lady, in a trembling voice.

CONCILIATE THEM: *gain their favor*

"Thou hast not come with weak womanly tears to disgrace thy name as a daughter of Britain," said one.

"Or to mar thy sacrifice as it is about to be offered," said another.

Guntra clasped her hands and raised her eyes appealingly. "I am a woman and a mother," she said, struggling to subdue her rising sobs, "I am a widow, too, and Jugurtha is my only son, the hope of my tribe and the light of my eyes. When he was vowed to the gods I had a husband, and the hope of other sons, but they have not been given me, and he is my only one."

"Thou hast a daughter," hastily interrupted a Druid.

"Norma is but a child, but Jugurtha is my stay; and, moreover, is anxious to gird on spear and target, and fight against the Romans," said Guntra, quickly. "It was that our Britain might be rid of the oppressor that I vowed him to our gods, but it may be he will rid it better by wielding the spear and battle-axe than yielding himself to the sacrifice."

"And thou wilt give thy young daughter instead," demanded the oldest Druid, who occupied a raised seat in the center, and was chief of the assembly.

The mother gave a shuddering start of horror at the mention of her sweet little girl in connection with that horrid wicker image, and that blackened spot that even now was within sight. Again

STAY: *support*

GUNTRA BEFORE THE SACRED COUNCIL

she raised her hands appealingly. "Oh, spare me one child!" she gasped, in agony. "My son may lose his life by a Roman javelin, and will you take my daughter likewise?"

Hard as the hearts of these Druids were, they could not but feel somewhat touched by the mother's earnest appeal.

"There is reason in what she says," remarked one: "Jugurtha is strong, brave, and fearless, he might inspire our warriors with fresh courage, and a successful attack might be made on the camp and colony of London. If this could be carried out, it would be better than sacrificing him to the gods, and another might be chosen in his place."

But several shook their heads at this proposal. "The gods accept not the vile and refuse: if Jugurtha is to fight the Romans, another equally dear and precious must be given instead, and that other is his sister."

"But if the gods take him while fighting, Guntra will lose both her children," said another, who had some sense of justice if not of pity. They would have been ashamed to own the latter, and yet a feeling closely akin to it stole into more than one heart as they looked at the tall white-draped figure standing before them with clenched hands and pain-drawn face, waiting to hear the doom of her children; for against that tribunal there was no appeal.

But it seemed that the council could not agree as to whether the little Norma should be taken in-

TRIBUNAL: *court*

stead of her brother, or whether his taking arms and waging war ceaselessly against the Romans should be counted as equivalent to sacrificing him to propitiate the favour of the gods.

Weary, heartsick, ready to faint with anguish of soul, Guntra stood patiently listening to the debate going on; but at length the council broke up without anything being decided, and the anxious mother was told that she must come again the following day to hear the decision, and receive the commands of the council.

As a highborn British matron, Guntra disdained to saw any signs of fatigue as she slowly turned towards her attendant warriors, who, in their sheepskins and war paint, stood like statues, awaiting the commands of their liege lady.

She silently motioned to them to follow her as she drew near, and without a word they fell into their places, wondering what could have taken place at the council to touch her so deeply; for in spite of all her efforts to suppress her emotion, the agony she was suffering was visible in her face.

Not a word was spoken until they reached the village, and then one of them more bold or more anxious to know what distressed her than the rest, ventured to say, "Will the brave youth Jugurtha join our warriors shortly?"

"I know not, I cannot tell," said the lady, quickly, and turning aside her head as she spoke; for

PROPITIATE: *gain for someone else*
LIEGE: *sovereign or lord*

silently and alone must this great burden of suspense be borne; and she was fearful of betraying any sign of it to these her devoted clansmen, who she felt were watching her.

It was more difficult to parry the questions of her son when she reached her home; for Jugurtha, in his anxiety to hear the result of her application to the council, had loitered near the village all day, mending his fishing-tackle, and amusing his beloved sister. Not that he had much fear of the result. He felt sure the lawgivers of the land would be only too glad to employ his strong arms against the common foe to refuse his request. He knew nothing of the heavy load of suspense and sorrow his mother had borne alone for years; that long since he had been destined for a very different fate, and the time for its fulfillment was now drawing near.

So it was with an eager, hopeful step he went out to meet his mother when he saw her approaching; and in his impatience he quite failed to see the pain so visible to others in her face.

"The matter is not decided, my son," said the lady, in a tone of forced calmness.

"Not decided!" repeated Jugurtha. "Do they hesitate to employ another warrior against our oppressors? Then I will myself go forth and avenge the wrongs of our people," said the young man, passionately.

"Hush, hush, my son! speak not so hastily," said the lady, in a tone of command; "you forget that *I*

PARRY: *evade or dodge*

am your chief as well as your mother," she added, "and that I must command you to gird on spear and target before you have the *right* to go out against our foes."

Jugurtha looked down abashed. "I have been overhasty," he said, in an humble tone; "but you will forgive me, my mother, and bid me fight for you against the Romans."

Guntra looked at her handsome, stalwart son bending before her, and longed to clasp him to her heart, but she feared to betray her secret by such unusual emotion, and so she contented herself with laying her hand fondly on his fair hair, and saying, "I know, my son, you will be willing to fulfill any command I may lay upon you, but you must likewise be obedient to the sacred council of the Druids."

Jugurtha did not reply. If the commands of the Druids agreed with his own wishes, he was willing to follow them; but so anxious was he to strike a blow against the Romans at their far-famed camp and colony of London, that he would not promise to forego this, even for the Druidical council; for he had already formed a plan of surprise in his own mind, which he felt sure must strike terror into the heart of every Roman in the country if he could only carry it out. He had hoped this was a council of war that had assembled today, for no tribe, however great their injuries might be, could go to war without the consent the council; but

ABASHED: *ashamed*

what had taken place he could not discover from
his mother, and so leaving her with little Norma,
he went out to try and learn something of its purpose from those who had accompanied her.

But they could tell him nothing save that their
chief had seemed deeply moved while speaking to
the Druids, and they had heard nothing of war being declared against the invaders.

"Then why was the council summoned?" asked
Jugurtha, quickly.

The old warriors shook their heads. If they
guessed they would not tell him; but one less cautious than the rest said, "You were the cause of the
council being summoned, my young brave."

Jugurtha stared, then smiled and shook his
head. "No, no," he said, "it was something of more
importance, I doubt not. My mother is to attend
the council again tomorrow, I hear; will you find
out what the subject of debate is, and tell me?" he
added.

The following day Guntra again set out with her
attendant warriors to the place of meeting, but
fearing lest a word should be overheard by them,
and reported in the village, she bid them halt some
distance beyond where they had stood the previous day, and went on alone to hear the decision of
the Druids concerning her son. She was not kept
long in suspense today. They had made up their
minds before she came, and warned her not to
waste words in questioning their wisdom, when

she should hear what had been decided. Jugurtha might become a warrior, and should at once be invested with his arms; but if he escaped the Roman javelins, and returned home alive, Norma was to be given up as a sacrifice to the gods.

The lady turned pale and shivered as she heard the decree, and was about to appeal to their pity to spare the sweet young life, but she was instantly silenced by the presiding Druid. *Pity!* what did he, a Briton and a Druid, know of pity? Guntra herself, woman though she was, ought to be ashamed of such a feeling.

Perhaps she thought it was unbecoming in a British matron to feel so deeply, for she walked away bowed, and looking as though all life had been crushed out of her, nor did she turn to summon her attendants to follow her when she reached them. But they knew their duty too well to linger behind when she had passed on, and with eager, anxious, wondering looks at each other they silently followed her back to the village.

Jugurtha met her eyes, as before, to know the result of her visit, and she told him part,—that he was at once to bear arms in defense of his country, which quite satisfied the young man, and he did not ask any further questions.

Little Norma was eagerly awaiting the arrival of her mother, to show her the curious face her brother had carved for her in a piece of wood, and she was not a little startled at being caught in her mother's arms, and strained passionately to her breast. She looked in her mother's face in surprise, and said, "What is it? is there a wolf coming?" for she remembered once when a wolf made his way into the village; every mother caught her child in her arms as soon as the alarm was raised, and she was about to raise her voice, and cry, "A wolf! a wolf!" when her mother stopped her, and carried her into the house.

"The wolf is not coming yet," said the lady, inwardly thinking that the council she had just left had been as pitiless in its decision as a wolf could be in its hunger.

"Will it come presently?" whispered the child, fearfully cowering in her mother's arms, as she seated herself on a pile of skins.

A savoury dish of field-mice had been prepared for Guntra, and was now brought in on a wooden platter, or shallow bowl, and set down before her. But she had no appetite today. She was conscious of but one wish,—to hold Norma in her arms, and feel the soft dimpled cheek pressed against her own. The thought of the child being a moment out of her sight was in itself misery to her now, for she might at any moment be taken away, and kept from her until the time of sacrifice arrived. She could even wish now, as she looked at the pretty rounded limbs, that she had not been so beautiful—that there had been some twist or contortion to mar their beauty, that

she had been lame or blind, and thus spared to
her.

Then she thought of her son, her brave noble
Jugurtha, falling a victim to the cruel Romans.
True, this would secure Norma, but it was a fearful price to pay for the life of one child with the
death of another. The thought of this so unnerved
her, that when Jugurtha came in some hours afterwards to tell exultingly of some feat of arms, instead of praising him for his skill and bravery, she
only shivered with apprehension as she thought of
his return from the fight with the Romans, and
how all exultation and joy would die out of his
heart when he heard of the fate of his little sister.

The young man was evidently disappointed at
his mother's silence, and not a little surprised.
That she should feel anxious for his safety never
entered his mind, for feelings of kindness or pity
were rarely shown, and being looked upon as
something to be ashamed of, were not much re-
spected, and so Jugurtha could not think his high-
born mother guilty of such weakness as an ordi-
nary British woman would be ashamed of, and yet
her manner towards him was very puzzling. At first
he thought Norma must be ill, for when the child
went to sleep, and was laid on the couch of skins,
his mother persisted in sitting beside her instead
of in the outer apartment; and when in the midst
of an exhortation to him to be diligent in learning
the use of the target, so that he might ward off the

javelin thrusts of the Romans, she stopped short, and again shivered as she looked down at the little girl sleeping at her side.

"Is Norma ill, my mother?" asked Jugurtha, anxiously, and bending himself over his darling sister.

His mother clasped her hands. "I would to the gods she were sick, even unto death," she uttered, with a cry of wild despair. The cry woke the child, and she started up in bed, while Jugurtha knelt at his mother's feet, and begged her to tell him what these wild words meant.

"Hush! hush! I am wild, I think these Romans will drive me wild," said Guntra more calmly, and anxious now to recall her incautious words.

But Jugurtha was suspicious that his mother was hiding something from him. "But, my mother, the Romans are not likely to attack us, are they? Why should you wish Norma was sick to death?"

"Why should I wish her to live, and these cruel oppressors in the land?" said Guntra, passionately. "Is a Briton's life so happy now that I should covet a long life for my child? No, no, Britain's happy days are over; our gods are angry, and will not help us, and we—we are growing weak and pitiful as little children."

Jugurtha thought his mother must be ill, and went out at once to bid one of their slaves prepare a decoction of roots and herbs for her, and then inquired whether any more of their cattle or crops

DECOCTION: *an extract obtained by boiling down*

had been carried off by the enemy, for this alone, he thought, could account for her extreme anxiety and this most unheard-of emotion. But nothing had occurred that day, the flocks and herds had been allowed to feed in peace, and not an ear of corn had been touched in the fields, and Jugurtha returned to his mother's chamber deeply anxious to discover what ailed her. But she was calm now, and only anxious to remove all suspicions from Jugurtha's mind. She spoke of a pain in her head, of the long walk to the Druids' council, of the loss her people had suffered in having their cattle driven off by the Romans,—of everything but the real cause of her trouble; that she carefully concealed, lest Jugurtha should throw himself recklessly into the hands of the Romans.

She succeeded at last in making her son believe it was the cares of her people and the heat of the weather that had for the time overcome her, and he resolved to apply himself with greater zeal than ever to learn the use of arms, that these enemies might be subdued, and his mother's heart set at rest concerning the property of her tribe.

CHAPTER III

THE ATTACK ON THE ROMANS

IN many a village of Britain preparations for war were being carried on throughout the livelong summer day during the next few weeks, but of all the warriors thus preparing for the fight, none were more earnest and industrious than the noble young Briton, Jugurtha.

His mother, as the head of the tribe, was likewise busy in consulting her warriors, issuing commands to her slaves, and making those general preparations for the attack on the Romans that the case demanded; but amid all these public cares her anxiety concerning the immediate welfare of little Norma never abated. If the child were out of her sight ten minutes she was restless and unhappy, and slaves were sent in search of her, and strictly commanded not to let her leave the house again.

Jugurtha was often puzzled by his mother's manner towards himself too. He was now to take her place as chief of his tribe, and lead on his warriors to the attack; and at one moment she urged him like a true British prince to shrink from no danger, to throw himself foremost into the camp of the Romans, and never surrender while he could hold a spear. Then again she would beg him with almost trembling earnestness not to throw his life away needlessly, to remember that she was a widow, and he the last of his noble race, and implore him not to fight recklessly even against the Romans, a charge Jugurtha could not understand at all, and which made him often look suspiciously at her.

At length the day was appointed for the tribes to meet, and receive the last commands of the Druids as to the line of policy to be followed in making the attack on Londinium.* Each tribe was led by its own chief, whose commands it was bound to obey, while the chiefs were equally bound to follow the directions of their priests and lawgivers. But alas for their discipline and unity! many of these tribes hated each other almost as fiercely as they did their common enemy, the Romans; and their sensitive pride was so easily wounded, that on the slightest provocation they were likely to turn their arms against each other instead of uniting against the common foe.

Jugurtha claimed the honour of leading the attack this time, for it was his tribe that had so sorely suffered lately from the marauding Romans; and, moreover, his long-thought-of plan had been submitted to the Druids and accepted by them, a fact

* LONDON
PROVOCATION: *reason for quarrel*
ALTERCATION: *heated argument*

he was not likely to forget, and which his warriors took care the other tribes should hear of; for they were not a little proud of their young deputy chief.

To obey the commands of their lawgivers was the duty of every tribe, but they were not bound to follow an upstart boy, who chose to place himself at their head, and they would not do it, they loudly declared. Some time was wasted over this altercation, but peace was at length restored, and led by a white-robed Druid, the Britons set out on their march towards London.

All sounds were hushed as they entered the wood that skirted the camp. The sun was setting as the wild, half-disciplined, but brave tribes of Britons pushed their way through tangled brakes, or struggled over patches of morass; but they halted not, though the wood grew denser and darker at each step, for the camp of Londinium must be reached before midnight, and the first blows struck while the sentinels were relieving the previous watch.

Jugurtha, in his ignorance of Roman discipline, judged that this would be a moment of confusion among the guards, and therefore the most favourable moment of attack, and everything had been planned—their march, or rather scramble through the woods, the point at which they were to issue from the sheltering trees, and the particular earthwork they were to scale—with this in view.

BRAKES: *thickets*
MORASS: *marsh or bog*
EARTHWORK: *wall built of dirt*

Slowly and silently paced the Roman guard around the earthworks and ramparts of their far-famed camp. Marcinius was on duty that night, and as he silently looked up to the starlit sky he thought of another guard he had kept under a noble Roman centurion under the skies of Syria. There were not many left of the grand old Roman type; but the soldier Cornelius was one of these, and Marcinius had loved to serve him as well as many another, among the hundred he command-ed. Then he thought of the wonderful vision that had been sent to his chief while they were quar-tered in the city of Cæsarea; and how through this vision he was sent with two household servants to the seaside town of Joppa, in search of a man who could make known to them all some wonderful news concerning them, as well as all men dwelling on the earth.

How well he remembered that two days' journey, and the venerable Jew who met him with courtesy instead of scorn, as was usual with the race! As an angel of God had he been to him as well as to Cor-nelius and his friends; and sorely had it grieved him to leave these dear friends on the shores of Syria, and travel to this distant barbarous Britain; but the brother of his chief had been sent to the camp of Eboracum,* and hither he had come to bring to his kinsman the good tidings of what God had done for Cornelius, and to bear letters and a roll of parchment like his own, containing

* YORK

CENTURION: *a commander of 80-160 men*

some of the sayings of the Lord Jesus Christ which His apostle Peter had treasured in his memory.

The scream of the bittern from the adjoining morass recalled the Roman soldier to his more immediate surroundings, and pausing in his steady walk to listen more attentively, he heard a slight rustle at a distance, which his acute ear told him was more than the night wind stirring the bells of the foxglove, or the fronds of feathery fern. Again he paced on, and again he paused to listen, and this time he felt sure that the long-expected attack was at hand. In a moment the alarm was given,—passed from sentinel to sentinel; quietly, but almost as quick as thought, a blast of trumpets awoke the echoes among the woods and hills; but while it was ringing the Britons had rushed to the ramparts, and scaling ditch and earthwork had fallen upon the Roman sentinels.

But they were prepared; Roman discipline was always alert, and ready for any emergency. Tall centurions led on their men to meet the furious onslaught; the eagle gleamed everywhere victoriously, and after a desperate fight, wherein it had been difficult to discern between friends and foes in the fitful gleam of torches, the Britons had been driven off.

When the sun rose the next morning, the Romans had already set to work to repair their defenses. A few wounded Britons had fallen into their hands, these would be examined by and by,

BITTERN: *a large bird that lives in marshes*

and if worth the trouble their wounds would be dressed, and they sent to one of the numerous slave markets in Rome.

"They are none of them worth much," grumbled one of the soldiers as he turned aside from viewing the captives; "there will scarcely be a sesterce apiece from such a lot as this. Why did you not take their leader, Marcinius? He would have brought something worth having; such limbs as his are worthy of being seen in the circus, and he might even have been trained as a gladiator. Why did you not take him instead of striking the spear from his hand?" he added, turning almost fiercely towards his companion.

Marcinius smiled. "It is not so easy to take a brave young Briton," he said, "I had enough to do to prevent him from carrying off our standard, for he seemed determined to have our Roman eagle as a trophy of the fight."

"By Castor and Pollux, you talk as if these wild Britons could fight as well as Roman legionaries!" he said, contemptuously.

"They would fight as well and even better than us, if they could forget their feuds with each other, and learn something of our Roman discipline, for they are fighting for the love of home and country, and we—"

"Because we are Romans, and the rightful masters of the world," interrupted the other. "What would this Britain be but a wild uncultivated

SESTERCE: *a Roman coin made of brass*
CIRCUS: *a circular arena for chariot racing, horse shows and staged battles*

morass but for us? We have made the great road leading from the coast to this camp of London. We have built these temples to Diana and Apollo. We have taught these people how to plant their corn, and would teach them other useful arts if they were less stiff-necked and proud."

Marcinius looked at the haughty face before him, and thought the Romans had little room to talk of other people's pride. He knew what this same Roman pride was, and how hard to subdue, but he was trying to subdue it,—to bring it into captivity to the gospel of Jesus Christ. But for this he would not have borne so meekly the taunt about allowing the young Briton to escape, for taunts that are half-truths are the hardest to be borne, and he knew he could have taken Jugurtha prisoner if he had pleased. But he allowed him to escape, although it was a clear loss of a thousand sesterces at the very least to him and his companions.

He would not let him take the Roman standard, he defended that, and repulsed every attack of the young Briton; but having done his duty, he did not forget that he served a God of love and mercy, even in that hour of strife, and shrunk from dooming that brave young heart to the protracted miseries of slavery.

But for this, Marcinius was likely to fall into ill odour with his companions; he knew already that some whispers had gone abroad that he did not worship the gods of Rome, and he was not so pow-

CASTOR AND POLLUX: *twin brothers in Greek mythology*
PROTRACTED: *long, drawn out*
FALL INTO ILL ODOUR WITH: *be offensive to*

erful at emptying a wineskin as most of his comrades, both grave faults in the eyes of a Roman
soldier, but the gravest fault of all was that Marcinius had been heard to object to the gladiatorial
shows, and had even said it would be better for
Rome if the Emperor closed the amphitheater. So
he would have to be careful how he treated these
slaves who had fallen into their hands, lest they
should think he wanted to cheat the Roman people of part of the spectacle to be provided at the
next feast of Ceres, when they would most likely
figure in the arena, with some fresh wild beast
from Africa.

The wounds of the soldiers were soon tended
with rough but kindly skill, but no one seemed to
think the Britons needed care and attendance.
They were carefully tied up to some posts that
they might not escape to their native woods again,
but the bravest of them could not but hope, in his
pain and anguish, that the great deliverer—death
—would soon free them from Roman bonds and
Roman cruelty, when they might enter the body
of some sweet-singing nightingale, and view at a
distance the home joys they had left to fight for
their country's freedom.

This was the brightest hope their Druidical
faith afforded them, but even this was in every
way preferable to being the bond-slave of a Roman, and at length one of the warriors resolved
to free himself, if death did not free him sooner,
for now that the day was advancing the pain of his

CERES: *the Roman goddess of agriculture*

undressed wounds became almost unendurable. Marcinius had not forgotten the British slaves, although he had not dared to relieve their torture, but now noting the restless agony depicted in their faces, he said to his companions in a tone of assumed carelessness, "They will escape you yet, if you are not careful, and be off to their native woods."

The soldier shook his head. "I have tied them fast," he said, "and they have no death-penny in their mouths to pay the ferryman to take them over the dark river."

"They would tell you they needed none; a nightingale of their own woods awaits each spirit as it is freed."

"Ah, then, we won't free them," said one. "Come, Marcinius, you are clever in the tending of wounds, look to these, that they may grace the next Roman games, and we will forgive your letting that boy warrior slip through your fingers."

This was just what Marcinius wanted. He had learned to delight in works of mercy, although a Roman soldier living by warfare; and in a few minutes he had brought a bowl of water, and was bathing the wounds of the captive Britons. But one of these brave patient warriors shook his head, and moved his arm away when he attempted to touch it.

"No, not water, but a spear," he said; "I am a Briton, and would be free."

"I would cut your cords and give you freedom if I dared," said Marcinius, pityingly; but the proud

Briton only looked more defiant and haughty as he detected the pity in his voice:

"I never asked a favour of man before, proud Roman," he said, "but I ask it now of you; drop your javelin but a moment within my reach, and I shall be free, and you cannot be blamed."

"Not so," answered Marcinius. "I suffered a young Briton to escape me this morning, and it will be said I am in league with your nation; besides, whither would you escape? The gods love not those—"

"I have nought to do with your gods," hastily interrupted the Briton; "each nation must worship its own, and leave all others. I hate your Roman gods," he added, fiercely.

"I love them not," quietly responded Marcinius, as he proceeded with his work of bathing and bandaging; "the God of heaven and earth, whom I serve, is greater than all the idols of the nations. You ask me for a spear to free yourself from the pains of the body, but whither would you go? We Romans love to decorate our tombs with a boar's head as a symbol of the long dark journey all must take. You believe that when your spirit has left your body it will but pass to that of an inferior animal; but the God whom I serve has shown that though the journey of death be dark, it is short, and there is brightness beyond—brightness of which we can have little idea now, only we know that pain and sorrow will be done away with and there will be no war and no slavery in that heavenly country."

SUFFERED: *allowed*

The Briton had forgotten to resist the process of dressing his wounds now, and listened with rapt attention.

"Go on," he said, when the soldier paused, "tell me more of this. Where is this heavenly country? How shall I find it? Will your Roman death-penny give me an entrance there?"

Marcinius shook his head. "The walls around this city are high, and cannot be scaled; there is but one door of entrance, and the right to pass through cannot be bought; an emperor's crown would avail him nothing there."

"Then there is no hope for a slave, and you are but mocking me," said the Briton, in a haughty tone.

"Nay, not so; there is hope for a slave as well as for a soldier like me," said Marcinius, quickly. "He who opened this door into the paradise of God will not sell the right to enter, but gives it freely to all who ask Him."

"Gives it?" repeated the Briton, in astonishment. "Are your Roman gods, then, so much more generous than our forest spirits?"

"He is not a Roman god, but the Lord God Almighty, the God who made heaven and earth,—the God of Britain as well as Rome and Syria."

But the half-wild warrior shook his head. "He has nothing to do with Britain," he said. "He will never be worshiped here. The Britons will be true to the forest spirits, though they be not true to us in driving back the legions of your Rome; *I* would hear more of the God *you* worship, but He is not, and never can be, the God of Britain," he added.

Marcinius sighed as he turned to another of the captives; it seemed probable that the Briton was right in what he said; these half-savage islanders were so proud, so firmly attached to their Druidical worship, and hated everything that came from Rome with such a fierce hatred, that it seemed impossible they could ever be won to the Christian faith; and yet Marcinius resolved to pray for them, as he did for Rome, although the hope for either was faint and feeble indeed.

The work of dressing the wounds of the captives was completed at last, and after a few words of kindness spoken to each, Marcinius returned to his companions, and prepared to take his place again as sentinel on the ramparts.

He hoped the captured Britons would be allowed to remain at this outpost for today, that he might have another opportunity of speaking to them, and relieving their sufferings; but shortly after he mounted guard the Prætor ordered them to be taken within the walls of London, where they would remain until their wounds were healed, and then be driven with more of their countrymen along the great road leading to the coast of Dover, and shipped to Rome for the supply of her slave markets.

PRÆTOR: *commander of the army*

CHAPTER IV

THE VICTIM'S ESCAPE

WEARY and dispirited, the defeated Britons made their way back through swamps and woods to the plain beyond; Jugurtha was, perhaps, the most sorely disappointed, the most deeply grieved at the failure of their enterprise, and instead of walking with head erect stepping proudly in the front, he lagged behind as they drew near the end of their journey.

The Druids had left them some time before, but Jugurtha had not noticed their departure, for he was too much occupied with his own gloomy thoughts to heed what was passing around him. Two of his dearest friends had been captured by the Romans, and would pass the rest of their days in slavery he well knew, and so instead of going back joyous and exultant with tidings of victory, as he had fondly and confidently hoped, he would have to tell of defeat and degradation, and bitter thoughts rose in his heart as he walked. He wondered how it was the Romans were always victori-

DEGRADATION: *disgrace*

ous wherever they went. Was it because the gods of Rome were more powerful than their own forest spirits? or was there a war waging now between these—the good and the evil fighting for the dominion of Britain, and in the turmoil of their own affairs they had not time to attend to mortal concerns?

This was the only solution of the mystery Jugurtha could arrive at, for the Druids had done all in their power to propitiate their mysterious deities he well knew, and a feeling of bitter resentment against them as the cause of their defeat began to arise in his heart. He began to mistrust them,—their power or their willingness to help their devotees, he scarcely knew which; and so it was with no very cordial feeling he heard from one of the warriors a little in advance, that the Druids were preparing to offer another sacrifice.

"It is of no use," said Jugurtha, in a hard tone, "our spirits are powerless against the gods of Rome, as powerless as we are against their impassable ranks."

They had reached the wide plain now, in the center of which stood the village, and a little nearer the grey towering moss-grown stones that witnessed their mysterious rites of worship. A company of white-robed Druids crowned with oak leaves, and each carrying an ivy-wreathed wand, was slowly advancing in an ever-widening circle towards the stones.

Scarce knowing what he did or why he did it, Jugurtha left his companions, and with rapid strides walked towards the spot. He wondered whether any sacrifice was to be offered today after their useless undertaking, and a half-jealous feeling, amounting almost to a desire to snatch the victim away, arose in his heart.

A few minutes brought him near enough to the Druids to see that the space was clear beyond, and he was just about to turn away before he should be observed by them, when from behind one of the huge granite blocks a little girl came shyly forward, flower-crowned, with fair curling hair falling over her white neck and shoulders.

"It is a shame to sacrifice so fair a child to our indolent gods," he exclaimed between his set teeth.

As the child came in sight the Druids commenced a low wailing chant in which was recounted the late defeat; but Jugurtha heard but a few words of this, for another look at the frightened face of the child beyond convinced him that it was his own sister—his little darling Norma, who was to be sacrificed. For a moment he stood motionless as if turned to stone, as immovable as those granite blocks. To him it seemed an hour that he stood staring blankly before him, unable to move a limb, but it was scarcely more than a minute, and then the lifeblood came surging back to his heart, and seizing the javelin that still hung at his side, he sprang forward, burst through the ranks of the

INDOLENT: *lazy*

astonished Druids, and catching little Norma in his arms, stood like some noble animal brought to bay, but determined to sell his life as dearly as possible.

For a moment there was a pause in the chant, which recounted all that the spirits had done for them in former times before the Romans came, but it was only momentary; a meaning look was exchanged between the priests, and again they took up the refrain, drawing nearer and nearer the circle, closing in as they came closer.

In a moment Jugurtha understood it all. He was on sacred ground, he too was doomed to die as well as his sister. Well, it should be so, if he could not save her, but at least he would try this first; and looking round on the narrowing circle of Druids as he clasped the child more closely in his arms, he noticed the point where two or three of the oldest and feeblest were together, and with a wild shout he bounded forward, dashed past them, knocking down one old man who attempted to stop him, and ran forward at once to the woods. There would be no safety for him in the village, for even his mother, dearly as she loved her children, would hesitate to shelter them now. It would be sacrilege of the deepest dye to withhold either of them from the gods now that they had once trod the sacred ground, been within the mystic Druidical circle.

DEARLY: *at a high cost*
SACRILEGE: *stealing something sacred*
DEEPEST DYE: *worst kind*

THE VICTIM RESCUED

So Jugurtha plunged through the morass, tore his way over brake and brier, with little Norma clinging frightened to his neck. She did not know from what she had escaped. The strange stern faces round had frightened her, and she was glad to see her brother, but she knew not that he came to rescue her from death, and wondered why he carried her to the dim shady woods, where they might at any moment meet with a wolf or a grim wild boar. Norma shuddered at the thought of the wolf, and said in a tone of fretful impatience, "What have you come here for? why don't you take me to Mother?"

"Hush! hush!" said Jugurtha, still plunging desperately forward, for he could hear sounds of pursuit even now. But little Norma's words had brought to his mind that there were other dangers to be avoided as well as capture by the Druids, and he became conscious that the direction he was taking led directly to a wolf's lair in the heart of the forest. He therefore struck off in another direction, almost unconsciously retracing the path he and his warriors had taken a short time before.

By degrees the sounds of pursuit died away, and nothing disturbed the calmness of the autumn day, but the occasional carol of some lingering bird, or the rustling of the leaves by some little pert squirrel in search of nuts or acorns. To watch these little creatures amused Norma when at length Jugurtha ventured to put her down, but the next minute she asked, "When shall we go back to Mother?"

Jugurtha started and turned pale. "Go back!" he repeated, and then he stopped, for he recollected there could be no going back but to die by those moss-grown stones in the plain.

Norma looked up at her brother's frightened face, and began to grow frightened too. "What is it? do you hear a wolf?" she whispered, creeping closer to him.

He roused himself, and tried to shake off the nameless horror that was creeping over him for her sake. "No, no, dear," he said, "there is no wolf. Look at that little squirrel, he has found a fine store of nuts; shall I go and get some of them for you?"

Jugurtha could be as tender as his mother when speaking to little Norma, and he took the child in his arms again and kissed her before going in search of the nuts. Nuts and acorns were plentiful just here, and Jugurtha soon gathered a large quantity and sat down to make a meal of them with his sister, for he was hungry now, and tired too—so tired that, after quenching his thirst at a little stream that meandered along a few paces off, as soon as he came back, he began telling his sister a story of the squirrels, when he fell asleep.

Norma watched her brother as he lay at her side, or the squirrels frisking about in the trees, and again fell to wondering why he had brought her there, instead of taking her home to her mother. She had not seen her mother today; for at sunrise she had been lifted from her couch of wolfskins and carried to a distance, where after some hours a flower-crown was brought and placed on her head; and she was taken to the sacred stones in the plain, and told to stay there. And there she had stayed until Jugurtha dashed through the white-robed priests and carried her off to the woods, for which she felt half-angry with him now.

But child as she was, her mother had already taught her some self-restraint, and that the first duty of a British maiden was to love the warriors who defended her country. It did not need the added honour of being a warrior, to make her love her brave, handsome brother; but it gave her more confidence in the wisdom of his proceeding now, and she would not waken him from his heavy sleep, even when the shadows of evening began to darken the wood.

The loud screech of the bittern at length awoke Jugurtha, and he started up with a look of wild terror in his face, until his eyes fell upon Norma and the faded crown of flowers that still hung in her tangled hair brought back to his mind all that had happened.

"I have slept long, little sister," he said; "you must he growing hungry again."

"No, I am not hungry," said Norma, "but I want to see Mother now; I have not seen her today."

Jugurtha turned aside his head as though listening to some sound, for he dreaded to tell the child he dare not take her home again; and then without noticing what she had said, he lifted her up in his arms and carried her on without a word.

"Are we going home now?" asked Norma, eagerly, putting her arms fondly about his neck.

"Hush, my darling! don't speak now; I am going to look for a place where we can sleep tonight, and then tomorrow we will talk."

Little Norma felt puzzled; she had never seen her brother so grave before. He was generally so merry and happy when they were out together, and always the first to propose going home, for fear his mother should be anxious about them.

It needed all the young Briton's caution now to avoid falling into the clutches of some cruel beast, or no less cruel Druid. Both sought and found shelter in caves or hollow trees, and in his search for a similar retreat he would have to assure himself that it was not already tenanted by one or other of his foes. Had he been alone he would have climbed one of the stately oaks, and disposed himself to sleep on one of its broad limbs as comfortably as on a couch of skins; but with Norma this was impossible, and the child was his first care now.

It was some time before he found a place suitable for his purpose, and more than one fierce growl was heard reverberating through the woods, that made Norma shudder and cling to him more

TENANTED: *occupied*
REVERBERATING: *echoing*

tightly; but he found a convenient shelter at last, and crept in with the child, feeling very thankful that neither wolf nor boar had as yet crossed their path.

He hushed little Norma to sleep in his arms as tenderly as her mother could have done it; he wanted the child to forget that her mother was not near her, but he was not likely to forget it himself. All the consequences of what he had done, now came to his mind for the first time. He had committed sacrilege in rescuing his sister, had dared the fury of the gods, and, what was no less to be feared, the Druids. He was an outcast now from home and friends, for none would receive him, and yet as he pressed his sister in his arms, and passed his hand over her fair tangled hair, he could not regret what he had done, though how they were to live now he could not tell.

For a few days, or even weeks, they might manage to subsist in the woods; but winter was drawing near, lean, gaunt wolves would be prowling round, and might kill and devour Norma while he was out in search of food. Then thoughts of his mother, and her anxiety concerning them, came to add to his distress, in the midst of which he quite forgot another enemy and another danger—his old foe, the Romans. Active bodily exertion, rather than the exercise of thought, was what the Britons delighted in; and sitting still in this woodland cave, Jugurtha soon found those superstitious fears he

SUBSIST: *remain alive*

had defied in the morning, creeping over him with tenfold power in the darkness and stillness of night.

The sighing of the autumn wind through the trees made him start and shiver, for it was not the wind only, but the angry moans of the forest spirits in his ears. Each leaf that rustled as it fell to the ground, each call of the bittern from the swamp, was an omen to him at night, a fearful whisper from his offended gods, who even now perhaps were summoning all their forces to torture and crush him and little Norma. He cared more for her than for himself. If he could have taken her home and placed her in her mother's arms in safety, he would willingly have come back to be the victim of the forest spirits, daring them to do their worst upon him, so that his mother and sister escaped unhurt.

But at length weariness overcame even his fear and terror, and he too fell asleep, and slept until the morning sunlight stealing into the cave awoke little Norma, who, in a fright at her strange surroundings, started from her brother's arms and awoke him likewise.

"Where are we?" exclaimed the child, rubbing her eyes as she sat up.

A tide of recollections came surging over Jugurtha's mind as he stretched himself. "You are safe, little sister," he said, quite forgetting that the child did not know she had been in danger.

"Safe!" repeated Norma. "Oh, Jugurtha, did the wolf come last night?"

"No, dear, no wolves came near our cave," said her brother, for he saw he must dispel this fear if possible.

"What are you going to do today?" asked the little girl.

"Pick up some nuts and acorns first," said Jugurtha. His fears of the night before had been greatly lessened by the morning sunshine, and he was disposed to make the best of their present position until something happened, though what that "something" would be, he could not tell.

"And after we have eaten the nuts and acorns what shall we do?" said Norma.

"You shall watch the squirrels while I cut you out some faces in sticks like you had at home," said Jugurtha. It was an unfortunate allusion just now.

Norma burst into tears. "I don't want any nuts, and I don't want you to cut sticks, I want my mother," she sobbed; and again and again came the cry, "I want my mother, I want my mother."

Jugurtha despised himself for the weakness, but he could not quite keep back his own tears at Norma's impassioned cry. He too wanted his mother almost as sorely as the child herself, and yet he knew that months or years might elapse ere they saw her again, even if they ever met.

But it would not do to tell Norma this just now. She must be pacified by some means for the

ALLUSION: *reference*

present, and by and by he hoped she would become reconciled to her life in the woods.

So by degrees the child was soothed into forgetfulness of her sorrow, and went with her brother to help gather the nuts and acorns for their morning meal, and then she paddled in the little stream and threw handfuls of water at him as he sat on the bank, and cut sticks into various devices for her amusement.

So the hours of daylight passed happily enough to Norma, but with the evening shadows again came the sobbing cry, "Take me home to my mother."

CHAPTER V

THE CAMP OF LONDON

ALL the Roman colony of Londinium was astir with the news that a new prefect had been appointed by the Emperor to govern Britain. The change in itself was not much indeed, but the triumphal march, the shows and games that would inaugurate his coming, were all-important to the camp and colony, who, bringing their Roman love of excitement and pleasure with them from the Tiber to the Thames, resolved to reproduce in Londinium all that was possible of the splendour and pomp likely to grace such a ceremony in Rome.

For a time the barbarian islanders were left to themselves, an immunity the Britons scarcely knew how to account for after their recent defeat. Had it been victory, they would have thought the Romans feared to make any further raids upon them, or even contemplated leaving the island; for the weeks of autumn passed, corn was cut and garnered for the winter, and not a marauder seen beyond the ramparts of London.

PREFECT: *a high Roman official*
POMP: *showy display*

The coming of the prefect had been delayed, day after day sentinels were posted at Dover, to watch for the imperial galleys, and dispatch news of their coming to the far-famed London, but there was an insurrection in Gaul, and the consular train was hindered in its progress to the opposite shore, circumstances which the new prefect could not prevent; and yet it would almost ruin his popularity with his new subjects he well knew.

But at length the long looked-for horseman was seen flying along the Dover road. The galleys were in sight at last, and all London turned out the next day to meet the triumphal car of the prefect. But his quick eye detected that the soldiers were not too cordial in their welcome, and he knew that some favour must be granted to pacify them at once. A few random words of a bystander concerning the islanders helped him to determine what this should be, and soon a proclamation went forth to the whole camp, that every soldier finding or taking a barbarian slave—which of course meant these free-born Britons—should hold him as his own property, or sell him in the slave market, the profit of the transaction to be exclusively his own.

This bait was not without its desired effect; prætors, centurions, and men loudly cheered their new governor, and a sharp lookout was maintained on the ramparts for any adventurous Briton coming near.

Winter was setting in now, and slaves were all

GALLEYS: *ships propelled by oars*
INSURRECTION: *revolt*
CONSULAR TRAIN: *procession of officials*

they were likely to get by a raid on the Britons, for their crops were garnered, and the flocks and herds kept nearer to the villages; and for some time the games and shows going on within the walls had more attraction for the soldiers than even a raid on their enemies.

Marcinius, however, had little taste for the brutal amusements of the circus now, and often went into the woods to study his precious piece of parchment, although he well-nigh knew it all by heart.

Wandering rather further than usual one day, he came to a small clearing, where, propped against a tree, wrapped in a wolfskin, sat a little girl. She was fast asleep, and looked so pale and wan, that Marcinius thought she must have wandered from home and lost her way in the woods. He wished he had not found her, or that he knew the tribe to which she belonged, that he might put her in the way of finding her friends again; for if she were left here some of his companions would be sure to find her before long, and he shuddered to think what her fate might be.

He was still looking at her, wondering what he should do,—take her home to his wife and child to be their slave, or leave her here where wolves or men—he scarcely knew which were more cruel— would inevitably find her before long.

The loud singing of a Roman song by several boisterous voices close at hand settled the matter at once, he took the child up in his arms, and at

CAR: *chariot*
GARNERED: *gathered*

the same moment a young Briton sprang forward. He glared fiercely at Marcinius, and attempted to seize the child, but the Roman held her fast, and clapping his hand upon the Briton's shoulder shouted, "Yield! thou art my prisoner."

It was the kindest thing he could do under the circumstances, for others were at hand, and he might find a more cruel master than him. But Jugurtha did not know this, Roman slavery was to him worse than death, and again he attempted to seize Norma.

But he was no match for the Roman soldier to-day. Anxiety for his sister, and want of food, had greatly reduced his strength; and as he saw several others spring forward through the underwood, he looked hastily round for his javelin, exclaiming, "Death will at least deliver me from Roman bonds." But his javelin was not at hand, and his head drooped forward as two others seized his arms.

"They are my prisoners," said Marcinius quickly.

"We won't dispute it, comrade," returned his companions. "March on with the cub thou hast taken, and we will bring on this young wolf. By the helmet of Cæsar he is as gaunt and lean as a wolf!" they exclaimed, looking at his pinched face and shrunken limbs.

Norma was too ill to do more than feebly cry for her brother as she was carried in the soldier's arms,—a cry that had the effect of quickening

Jugurtha's steps more effectually than the goading taunts of his merciless guards. Marcinius was scarcely envied his capture; a sick child and a half-starved youth would not fetch much in the slave market, and to keep them for any length of time would be a most unprofitable piece of business at the present high price of provisions.

In his misery and degradation Jugurtha had but one wish, and that was to be near Norma. Despair had settled down upon him before his captors came, and the most he could hope for, was that some prowling starving wolves would find them out and end their lives at the same time. He could not kill the child, and he would not kill himself and leave her to perish slowly by starvation; and the thought of the misery to which he had brought her, and how his noble mother had been robbed of both children in one day, made him almost sorry he had saved her from the Druid's knife. Truly the gods had been avenged, but they might have saved him from Roman slavery, he thought, and kept the vengeance in their own hands.

The walk to the camp well-nigh exhausted Jugurtha's feeble strength, for he too was suffering from fever and ague as well as Norma, and when at last the gate was reached and they paused to gain admittance, he sunk down helpless between his guards. They were about to strike him with their spears as they would an ox, but Marcinius interposed.

GOADING: *prodding*
AGUE: *a disease marked by fits of chills, fever and sweating*
INTERPOSED: *intervened*

"Thanks, comrades, for thus burdening your-
selves with my concerns," he said, courteously;
"I can trust the Briton to follow me now, since I
carry the child;" and he looked down pityingly at
Jugurtha as he said this. The words were spoken
in Latin, which the young Briton could not understand, but he comprehended the pitying look, and
that the Roman carried Norma as tenderly as he
could himself, and he struggled to his feet again,
determined to follow his sister. They were hardly
worth capture, he knew; and had he fallen into the
hands of another tribe of Britons with whom his
own were at war, an end would soon have been put
to their lives, and so he was surprised that Marcinius should take so much care of a chattel of so
little value as Norma was now.

His comrades in the camp were evidently of
the same opinion, and jeered him not a little for
his pains. One tall centurion wanted to persuade
him to leave the child outside, telling him his
wife would not thank him for such a burden as
that. But Marcinius only smiled as he shook his
head, and looked down tenderly at the little girl,
who had sobbed herself to sleep in his arms; and
Jugurtha, seeing that look, almost forgave him for
capturing them, since there was hope of relief for
Norma at last.

They had not far to walk when once they had
passed the ramparts, and Jugurtha followed the
soldier into a small house that to him looked like

CHATTEL: *slave*

a palace rather than a soldier's cottage; for Marcinius and his wife had gathered round them many of the comforts to which they had been accustomed at Rome. The court into which they first entered was hung with various, and some very elegant weapons, taken by their owner in his different campaigns in Europe and Syria. There were likewise several small statues disposed among shrubs that looked poor and dwindling in this northern clime; and a couch covered with a rich shawl of colours, so gorgeous, that to Jugurtha's unaccustomed eyes it looked only fit to be gazed at from a distance, and not to be touched by mortal hands.

On this shawl, however, Marcinius laid little Norma; and motioning Jugurtha to watch by her side, went in search of his wife. The young Briton needed no second bidding to approach his sister, but still he looked doubtfully at the shawl, the deep crimson of which showed up in such strong relief the white emaciated arms and thin wan face resting on its folds.

"Where am I?" said the child, with a little stifled cry, as the soldier moved away.

"Hush, darling! I am here," said Jugurtha, tenderly, sitting down on the mosaic pavement, and taking her hand.

She opened her eyes with a look of frightened wonder, and fixed them inquiringly on the myrtles and oleanders.

CLIME: *climate*
EMACIATED: *wasted away*

"They don't grow in the woods," she said,—for young as she was, she knew every plant that grew in her native forests.

"No," said Jugurtha, sadly, "we are not in the woods now."

"Are we in the home of the forest spirits?" whispered Norma, looking fearfully at one of the statues.

Jugurtha was not surprised at the question, for he too had started as he came in, thinking that these must be the pale cold gods he had worshiped afar off, until he remembered this was but a Roman soldier's house.

"No, they are not the forest spirits," said Jugurtha; "they are the gods of Rome, I expect."

"The gods of Rome?" repeated Norma.

But at that moment the curtain at the end of this small *atrium* or open court was drawn aside, and the soldier came back, accompanied by a matronly-looking woman, evidently his wife.

Jugurtha rose instinctively, for he had been trained to pay every mark of respect to his mother, and this woman, Roman though she was, reminded him of her. Then, too, he had not seen a woman for weeks—not since he had left home on that fatal enterprise against this very fort,—and the sight gladdened his heart as he looked at little Norma, and thought how much she needed a woman's tenderness and womanly skill to cure her of her sickness.

Marcinius looked surprised that the fierce young Briton should receive his wife so humbly and courteously, for, looking at him now, he recognized the bold huntsman who had called him a "dog" for trespassing on the forest ground.

"My wife will attend to the wants of the child," he said, in the Briton's own language,—for he had managed to learn this from the numerous slaves brought to the fort.

Jugurtha started as he heard his own language spoken. He recognized Marcinius then as the soldier whom he had insulted a short time before, and he doubted not but that the Roman recognized him, and would take a full and bitter revenge.

In a moment all the fierceness of his character, that sickness had weakened but not subdued, sprang into full activity. Springing to the couch where Norma lay, he placed himself before it, and though unarmed, attempted to strike Marcinius.

"Not one step nearer, Roman," he shouted, glaring at him with deadly rage. "Do what you will with me, but lay not a finger on her."

The matron had shrunk back in alarm as Jugurtha sprang forward.

"Oh these savage barbarians!" she cried, retreating behind the curtain. "Marcinius, send them to the slave market."

"Peace, woman!" said her husband.

"Yes, yes, send us to the slave market," said Jugurtha, in a tone so imperious that one might have thought Marcinius was his slave.

The proud Roman chafed inwardly, but he would not let it be seen.

"You know not what you ask," he said in a quiet tone, keeping at a little distance from the couch.

Norma began to cry in her fright at the strange scene.

"Oh, Jugurtha, why didn't you take me home to Mother?" she sobbed reproachfully.

Jugurtha turned to soothe the child, and Marcinius said, in a kind and gentle voice,—

"Do not be afraid, little one; you will find a mother here, if I mistake not;" and he ventured a step nearer as he spoke.

But the young Briton glared at him like an angry panther.

"Beware, Roman!" he shouted; "the strength has not quite forsaken my right arm;" and he held it up menacingly as he spoke.

Marcinius knew not what to do for the best, and retired for a few minutes to consult with his wife as to the best mode of proceeding; for he could see that both his captives were half-famished for want of food, and yet the proud obstinacy of the Briton would not let him submit to having his sister moved to where a meal had been hastily prepared for them.

The Roman matron was afraid of her slave too; but Marcinius knew this fear to be groundless, for he saw that Jugurtha was too brave a man and too noble a foe to injure a defenseless woman, and so

CHAFED: *was annoyed*
GROUNDLESS: *without basis*

at last he resolved to leave it for his wife's wit to devise a plan for the relief of the captives, for the water-clock reminded him that it was time for him to return to his duties on the rampart.

"Briton," he said as he passed through the *atrium*, "I leave you to my wife. You have a mother whom you love, and in her name I charge you not to injure another woman."

Jugurtha's pale cheek flushed.

"Britons do not fight with defenseless women," he said, proudly; "they leave such work as that for their foes the Romans."

Marcinius would not heed the stinging speech, although it brought the hot blood to his cheek, and his hand instinctively grasped the weapon at his side. Jugurtha noticed the action, and hated himself for having uttered such a taunt, when it could not be retaliated. He knew if such an insult had been offered to him he should have demanded instant satisfaction. Springing after Marcinius, he touched him on the shoulder before he could leave the house.

"Roman, give me the use of yonder javelin," he said, pointing to one hanging on the wall, "and you may wipe out the insult in my blood and in fair fight."

"Fair fight!" repeated the Roman. "Would it be a fair fight when you are weak and I am strong? Wait awhile, Briton, until you have recovered strength, and then if you wish it we will talk of fighting."

Unconsciously Marcinius had stung the proud

SATISFACTION: *righting of an offense through a duel*

Briton as deeply as he had himself been stung. To be reminded of his weakness was like telling him he was despised, and he crept back to Norma feeling that he was indeed weak and powerless; for the temporary excitement had forsaken him, and he sank down on the floor utterly exhausted.

From her post of observation behind the curtains the Roman matron could see all that passed, and pity very soon took the place of fear when she saw Jugurtha lying helpless on the floor. Seizing a cup of wine that stood on a table near, she hastened into the *atrium*, and raising the young Briton's head, put the cup to his lips. He swallowed a little, but wine was nauseous to one who never drank anything but water, and he looked keenly into her face, wondering whether it was poison he had swallowed. She smiled, and he felt somewhat reassured; but he pushed her arm aside as she attempted to put the cup to Norma's lips.

Neither understanding the language of the other, it was some time before he could make her understand that they wanted water; but she comprehended the meaning of his signs at last; and when this was brought, she contrived to induce him to take some food as well; and shortly afterwards both he and Norma fell asleep, to dream they were once more free to roam through their native woods, but to awake and find themselves Roman slaves.

CHAPTER VI

THE GOSPEL OF LOVE

JUGURTHA did not know how long he had slept, but he awoke with a sense of weakness and exhaustion he had never experienced before. Pushing aside the leopard-skin with which he was covered, he saw that he was in a little dimly lighted room, whose open door—which likewise served as a window to admit what little light there was—gave him a glimpse of the hall, or *atrium*, where he remembered having fallen asleep.

In a moment his old suspicion of the Roman soldier returned. Why had they moved him? and where was Norma? for she was not to be seen. He did not stay to ponder upon these questions long, but crept to the door as quickly as his weakness would allow, in order to gain a better view of the hall, and see if Norma was still lying on the couch.

A strange sight met his view. On the mosaic pavement lay several eagle-crowned helmets and iron shields, while their owners stood or sat round

Marcinius, who was reading aloud from a roll of parchment. To see soldiers quietly listening with such rapt attention was in itself a wonderful sight to Jugurtha, but his surprise was increased by seeing two of his countrymen—friends of his own, who had been captured in the late unfortunate expedition against the Romans—likewise of the company. They, too, were listening with the same deep attention as the Roman soldiers, and for a moment a feeling of bitter hatred against them arose in the young Briton's heart. "They love not their native land, or they could not thus sit in peace with our enemies," he hissed between his clenched teeth. He almost hoped they might hear what he said, but they were too deeply engrossed with the reader to notice anything but the words that fell from his lips.

In a few minutes the parchment was rolled up and slipped into its case, and then the whole company knelt down while Marcinius prayed. Jugurtha looked round now for the Roman's God, but he could see nothing. Marcinius had turned his back to the statues, and raised his eyes to heaven —for the hall was open in the center, and looking up, Jugurtha could only see the leaden clouds passing over the sky; and yet as he listened, the young Briton looked round again, for the prayer was offered in his native language; and Marcinius spoke as though the God he prayed to, was there in the very midst of them. Then the British maiden

A STRANGE SIGHT

and her brother, who were sick almost unto death, were pleaded for, that God would teach them to know Himself before they died.

Jugurtha did not listen to any more. What could it mean? They thought he and Norma were both likely to die, and yet instead of turning them out to perish of cold and hunger, they took care of them as though they were profitable slaves, and even prayed that their God would show them some favour too. Truly these Romans were a strange people, and must worship a strange God, he thought.

But anxiety to know more about his sister soon took the place of these thoughts; and as the little company arose and began to put on their helmets, he made a slight noise to attract the attention of Marcinius, who, as soon as he heard it, came forward to inquire what he wanted.

"Nay, nay, this is wrong," he said, in a tone of gentle expostulation, "you must not lie here on the cold stones, or the fever will return upon you again;" and lifting the young Briton in his arms, he carried him back to his skin-covered couch and wrapped him up again.

Jugurtha was inclined to rebel at being dealt with in this way, but one of his friends, who had followed Marcinius into the room, came to the side of the bed, and kissing him fondly, begged him not to get up again. Jugurtha stared at his former companion as he laid his hand upon his

EXPOSTULATION: *protest*

shoulder. Was the world turned upside down, and had the wolves lost their liking for blood, that a fierce Briton should show affection?

"What is it? what has happened?" asked Jugurtha, as soon as he could speak.

"You have been ill, and are very weak," said the slave.

"Yes, yes; but you?" said Jugurtha; "does life in the Roman camp change a Briton's nature?"

His countryman shook his head, and with a faint smile answered, "No, Jugurtha, the Spirit of the living God alone can do that."

"Who is this God?" asked the invalid.

"Thou shalt hear of Him by and by," answered Marcinius. "Validier, thou must go now," he said, turning to the slave; "a Christian must not be less diligent about his lawful business, and the centurion will be returning shortly from the ramparts, and need thy attendance."

Without a word of demur the slave turned away, a bright smile illuminating his face as he looked back to nod adieu to Jugurtha. Before he had left the house the sonorous bray of Roman trumpets summoned Marcinius likewise to his duty, for he was a decurion, or captain of ten, and he knew that if he were unpunctual, his men would soon grow remiss in their duty too; and so not even for the sake of saying a few words to Jugurtha would he linger, but putting on his eagle-crowned helmet he hurried away.

DEMUR: *hesitation*
ADIEU: *goodbye*
SONOROUS: *rich, impressive*

But Jugurtha was not left alone long; the Roman matron soon came in, bringing him some nourishing food. In his unconsciousness Jugurtha had eaten this before, but it was distasteful to him now, and he asked for acorns, his usual diet when at home in his native village. But his nurse could not understand his request, and at last, seeing he persistently pushed the food aside, she thought it must be drink he wanted, and fetched a draught of milk. This he drank, but still refused the food; until at last, thinking the sight of his sister would perhaps cheer him, the kind-hearted matron went and fetched her.

She looked only like a bundle of shawls and skins lying in the woman's arms, so carefully had she been wrapped up to guard her from the cold as she crossed the hall; but as soon as her face was uncovered and she saw Jugurtha she uttered a low cry of pleasure, and held out her arms towards him.

He would have sprung out of bed to reach her if she had not been brought and laid down at his side. But after the first transport of pleasure was over, Norma wanted her nurse near her too. "Jugurtha, she has been so kind to me," said Norma,—"almost as kind as my mother," she added in a whisper. Then turning to the Roman matron, she said, "My brother will love you by and by, and he will learn to speak in your tongue. Will you let Valeria come and see him now?" she asked.

REMISS: *careless*

Valeria was the soldier's only child, and about Norma's age, so that a friendship had sprung up between these two, which greatly helped towards the good understanding between Norma and Valeria's mother. The little girl was allowed to come in and look at her father's slaves as they sat rejoicing in each other's presence; but the excitement soon proved too much for both of them, and Norma was willing to be carried away again, and Jugurtha let her go without resistance now that he knew she was kindly treated. But the food that had been prepared for him he could not or would not eat yet, and still craved for his native acorns instead.

The Roman matron scarcely knew whether it was an invalid's whim or the native obstinacy of his character that made him refuse to eat the food prepared for him but in either case it troubled her, for she knew not where to get acorns in London; and for anyone to go into the woods beyond the ramparts was dangerous now, as several parties of armed Britons, and more than one war chariot had been seen lately in the neighbourhood, and therefore it was known an attack was meditated, and parties were lying in ambush.

Marcinius explained this to Jugurtha when he returned a few hours afterwards. The young Briton's eyes glistened with delight at the news. "I would that I were free and could strike a blow against the eagles of Rome too," he said, with a deep-drawn sigh as the smile faded from his pale face.

"Shall I tell you of a better freedom than that of Britain?" said Marcinius, seating himself by the side of his couch, and holding the wooden platter with some food on it.

Jugurtha looked disdainful. "A *better* freedom than that of our own forests! that cannot be," he said, still pushing the food aside.

But Marcinius pressed him to eat, promising him some acorns for the following day if they could be got; until at last, touched by the kindness of his master, he ate what had been prepared for him, and then asked more quietly what he meant by a "better freedom than that of Britain." "Is it better than Roman freedom too?" he asked.

"Yes, as much better than—"

"Then I will hear of it," interrupted Jugurtha, "for I have heard the Romans are proud of their freedom, although they enslave all other nations."

"Yes, we Romans are proud," said Marcinius, with something of a sigh; "but do you not remember the question you asked your countryman this morning, and his answer?"

"That the Spirit of your God changed a Briton's nature," said Jugurtha.

"Yes; and, thank God, He can change a Roman's nature too," said Marcinius.

"And is it this you spoke of as freedom?" said Jugurtha, wonderingly.

"Yes, for it frees us from the curse of sin; and the power of Satan, and the fear of evil spirits and false gods."

"Is your God greater, then, than the forest spirits whom I have offended?" asked Jugurtha,—"greater than Thor, whom our bards sing of as mighty in war, and terrible in his anger against mortals?"

"Yes, the God whom I serve is the Lord Almighty, the King of heaven as well as earth."

"And this great King, this mighty God, will give His Spirit to soldiers and slaves!" said Jugurtha, in a tone of surprise.

Marcinius remembered the scornful contempt with which the young Briton received this announcement before, and especially the news that He was a God of love, and he almost hesitated to speak of this again lest he should provoke another similar outbreak. But Jugurtha's next words showed that he had not forgotten what was spoken in the woods.

"Is it your God who teaches you to treat your slaves so differently from all others? If another tribe of my people had found me, they would have left me to perish when they found I was likely to prove a burden."

"And I might have done the same a few years ago, but while I was in Syria I heard of One who loved all men, whether Syrian, Roman, or Briton, —loved them better than life itself, for He died for them,—died that they might live, not merely in love with others in this life, but in the next, that they might have fullness of happiness and joy such as we can never taste on earth."

BARDS: *traveling poets*

"And this One who came was your God!" said Jugurtha, wonderingly. "Did you see Him?"

"No, I did not, but I saw and talked with one who knew Him well—who was with Him when He made the blind to see, and the deaf to hear, and the lame to walk."

"What is the name of this God?" asked Jugurtha, —for now that he was weak and suffering, he could listen to the story of One who was kind and compassionate, without scorn or contempt.

"The Lord Jesus Christ, God's only Son and only equal; there is no other God in heaven or on earth, for others that men worship are but vain idols, the work of men's hands."

Jugurtha listened, and pondered for some minutes in silence, but at length he said,—

"Your God taught you to be kind to slaves, even when they were likely to be useless; He, too, must be kind,—different from Thor or our forest spirits."

"He is different; He desires not to make men dread and fear Him, but to serve Him from love, and to teach His love by being kind to all men."

Marcinius thought he had said enough for once,—enough to set Jugurtha thinking; and so he went in search of his wife to inquire after Norma, and enjoy a little pastime with Valeria, for the soldier was very fond of his little daughter.

What he should do with his slaves when they got well, as they now seemed likely to do, he scarcely knew; he shrank from the thought of sending them to the slave market, and yet his means would scarcely allow him to keep them. To follow his own inclinations in the matter would be impossible, for he would like to have taught them both the Christian faith, and then set them free to carry it to their fellow-countrymen. But even if this had not been against the laws of Rome, he knew enough of Jugurtha's story to understand that it would be unsafe for him to come within range of a Druid's arrow or a fellow-countryman's spear, so that he must be protected from the persecution of the Britons as well as from the cruelty of the Romans.

Little Norma he had almost decided to keep, for the present at least, as a companion to Valeria; for the British child had shown such an aptitude in learning the Latin tongue, and was so docile and patient in spite of her illness, that he had already begun to love her; and besides, as he reflected, the perils of slavery were much greater for this gentle daughter of Britain than for the young warrior.

It was almost a relief to come back to the thought that neither could be sent away at present, that Christian duty demanded that he should feed and tend them both until they grew strong, although in the case of Norma the duty was far more pleasant than it was with her brother.

As he went into the inner chamber, where Norma was lying on a couch, and Valeria sitting by her side, he heard the little Briton softly repeating the words of a Christian hymn in Latin, which he knew he should be called upon to translate into her own tongue; for it was in this way Norma was learning the language of the conqueror of her land.

Valeria heard the rattle of his armour before she saw him, and immediately sprang up with the request, "My father, will you not tell Norma in her own tongue all this hymn means? she whispers it as softly as her own nightingales sing. Oh, my father, if these blue-eyed Britons were but Christians!" she added, clasping her hands and raising her eyes to heaven.

"We must pray for them, my Valeria," said her father, laying his hand on her head; "we know that our Father in heaven loves them more than we can do, and desires that they should know His love."

"But they are so fierce and cruel—oh, so cruel!" added Valeria, with a shiver.

"But our God is almighty," said Marcinius; "and if His power can bend the heart of a Roman, it can change that of a Briton;" and he wondered whether this religion of love, that in its very nature was opposed to all a Roman's ideas of pleasure, as well as a Briton's superstition, would ever conquer the one or the other. He hoped, he believed, it would; but sometimes the hope grew very faint, and his faith well-nigh failed, as he thought of what he had seen in the city of palaces on the Tiber, and what he had heard here in the green plains of Britain.

Valeria had heard of the awful human sacrifices that were sometimes offered by these Britons, but she was too young when she left Rome to remember the scarcely less awful gladiatorial shows, where slaves and captives taken in war were set to fight with wild beasts, or rather to be torn to pieces by them—for such unequal combat could not be called a fight—in the presence of the Emperor and all Rome's highest and most refined people; patrician and plebeian vying with each other in their eagerness to witness this cruel slaughter of men, either by the paw of wild beasts or by the swords of their fellowmen.

It was not strange that Marcinius should sometimes almost doubt whether this new religion would make its way in the world. None of earth's great and mighty ones believed in it; many had not heard of it, and if they had, would have derided it; for a few outcast Jewish fishermen were its principal teachers, and they had no schools of philosophy, like Plato, to attract the attention of the wise.

When Marcinius thought of all this—the weakness of the means, and the greatness of the task—and for a moment forgot that this new faith differed from all others in this—that it was divine, he was ready to give up hope for the world, until he remembered the most precious words of his scroll, "God is love."[1] With that thought, hope for the world, bad as it was, would again dawn in his

---

[1] I JOHN 4:8

PATRICIAN: *the upper class in ancient Rome*
PLEBEIAN: *the middle class in ancient Rome*

heart. Did not God love the world? and did He not send His Son to redeem it? and, having redeemed it unto Himself, would He not break the power of Satan by the almighty power of love, as the ice is melted by the genial rays of the morning sun? Gradually as the sun rose would the truth and love of the gospel rise in influence and power; and, in this little world of the Roman camp, Marcinius resolved that one beam at least should shine.

GENIAL: *pleasant*

CHAPTER VII

THE BEREAVED MOTHER

WE must now go back in our story to the day when Norma was rescued from the Druids, and carried off to the woods by Jugurtha. In his precipitate flight from the priests, and those whom they had summoned to assist them in the pursuit, he had unconsciously committed a second sacrilege in entering the sacred grove where alone the Druids might tread the greensward, and walk beneath the giant oaks. He did not know that he had so trespassed on the domain of his gods, but the Britons in pursuit did, and paused in horror, not daring to venture beneath those trees, and fully expecting to see the fugitive fall to the ground, struck by the vengeance of those spirits he had thus dared to insult.

But Jugurtha fled on, never slackening his speed, or showing any inconvenience from his sacred surroundings, and the Britons looked at each other, and then at the Druids, as they followed more slowly with their harps and wands.

PRECIPITATE: *hasty*
GREENSWARD: *grassy area*

"He has escaped," said one, "escaped even the fury of the gods."

"But not of the Druids," said a white-haired, stern-looking old man, whose character for sanctity was spoken of in every tribe. He had his dwelling, or rather, resting-place, in this very grove, for through all the cold of winter no roof ever sheltered that hoary head, and from sunrise to sunset no food or drink ever passed his lips. Animal food he never tasted; the acorns of his native oak, with a draught of water from the bubbling stream that wandered through the wood and crossed the sacred grove, was all that he allowed himself to eat. But for this reputed sanctity, he demanded the right to rule his brethren, the priests and bards, as well as the people of the village. He was cold, proud, and pitiless, and none dared offend him. It was his voice in the council that had decreed Norma should be taken as a sacrifice instead of her brother, and he was not one to stand by and let his victims escape, without making an effort to stop them.

For a moment he paused at the entrance of the grove, then rapidly passed on to a hollow tree, from whence he drew a bow and arrows, and the next minute one of these feathery messengers of death was whizzing through the air after the fugitives. But clever marksman as the Druid was, his aim was wrong for once, and instead of Jugurtha falling with a shriek of pain to the ground, the

SANCTITY: *holiness*
HOARY: *white with age*

arrow lopped off a piece of mistletoe, and before the half-scared Druids could rescue it, the white-berried parasite was seized by a wild boar who came breaking through the sacred enclosure in search of food.

A loud groan ran through the group of Druids as they saw what had happened, and an ill-defined sense of coming trouble seized the warriors standing outside the sacred precincts. Gloomily they picked up their skin-covered shields, and slowly retraced their steps towards the village. Their gods were offended with them, and would very speedily have their revenge. The Romans would be upon them before the present moon had run its course. Their flocks and herds would be driven off, and their crop of corn mildewed. All this would happen —must follow what they had just witnessed—and so it was with no song of rejoicing they went back to their homes to greet wives and mothers; but slowly, sadly, and silently they passed over the plain, and crept into their huts to tell the woeful tidings of defeat and disaster.

Ill news traveled then as it does now, and their defeat by the Romans was already known, as well as some vague report about the escape of Norma and her brother, but no one ventured to ask about this, for fear it should be thought they sympathized with the escape of the little girl, which would be a crime almost as great as Jugurtha himself had committed.

Not even her mother, anxious as she was to know the fate of her children, dared to ask a question about them, but she listened with straining ear and bated breath to every whisper that went on around her, and from these stealthily uttered words she learned that her darling had escaped the Druid's knife and fire, and his poisoned arrow too, and was borne off in safety by her brave brother. How she loved Jugurtha now, when she thought of his heroic deed, and how her heart bled for them both as she thought of their banishment from home and friends, through the pitilessness of the Druids and their vengeful gods.

But whatever Guntra might think concerning her children, their names never passed her lips; she listened attentively to all she could hear, often creeping into her hut with noiseless footsteps to overhear the conversation of her slaves, hoping in this way to glean tidings of her children; but she never asked a question. Outwardly this British princess grew more proud and cold, indulging in no grief for the loss of her dear ones, but wholly occupied with the public cares and duties of her tribe, and none guessed the thoughts and emotions of her motherly heart.

The day following the flight of Jugurtha and Norma one of the bards had brought his harp, and summoning the villagers to listen to his song, had recounted to them all that had happened. "It is the will of our gods that this should be," he sang, "for they are great and mighty, and delight in war. They will bring the Romans here to feast upon your cattle, and carry your children into slavery. The wolves shall come and tear down your houses, and lightning and rain shall blight your corn. All this will our mighty gods do, because they are offended—because the rightful sacrifice was withheld."

Guntra, as she listened to the weird, wild song, and the soft notes of the harp, felt her heart almost stand still with horror and fright at the prophetic words; for none in all the crowd doubted but that their bards were inspired with the spirit of their gods, when they sang such strains as these. Silently she turned away, not daring to look into the scared faces of her people, for she alone was guilty in bringing this curse upon them. She had withheld her son from being sacrificed, vainly thinking his life could be more profitably given to fighting the enemies of her country, and helping her to rule the tribe. She had grudged giving Norma, too, because she was beautiful and loving, as though the gods did not understand this! Of course they comprehended this weakness of her heart, and they had punished it too, by carrying off both her children.

Hard, cold, cruel faith! No wonder that this British matron grew hard and cold too—hard as her own warriors, pitiless as her stern teachers,— for there was no joy or happiness for her in this life, and no hopes to brighten the prospect of another.

But although joy and happiness had fled from her life, duty still remained, and her duty to her people she would perform at all costs. With her own hands she helped to cover the wicker shields or targets with half-dressed wolfskins, or prepared the sharp-pointed stone spearheads; for if the Romans meditated an attack upon her tribe, they would at least meet them like Britons, and sell their lives as dearly as possible. She herself had never been out to battle with them yet, but she had her war chariot prepared, the deadly scythes at the axletrees sharpened in readiness, for she herself would be their leader in resisting the coming attack.

But day after day passed, and nothing was seen of the dreaded Roman eagle. Sentinels were posted in various places to give timely notice of the approach of the enemy, but no enemy came. Their flocks and herds grazed undisturbed by the bray of trumpets; their corn ripened, and gave promise of a plentiful harvest, and there was no sign of blight or mildew, or its being struck by lightning.

At first the poor bewildered people were afraid to attempt gathering it in, for fear they should be destroyed in the attempt, since a curse had been pronounced against it, but their chief entertained no such fears. She had no hope in life, and therefore no fear; since her children had been taken, she cared little what became of herself, and so she would dare the curse and fury of the gods by cutting down the first sheaves. In her secret heart she had begun to doubt their power now, and she was rather glad than otherwise of thus putting them to the test, so she boldly marched forth in her long white robe, and a heavy bracelet of gold on her arm—the one insignia of her office as chief of the tribe—up to the hillside field of ripening grain, and there, amid the breathless silence of all her people, she cut down sheaf after sheaf until her arms were full of golden treasures. Then she held them forth saying, "Come, come, and let us cut the corn that the sunshine hath ripened, that we may not starve when the snow covers the earth."

With a glad shout of triumph the warriors leaped into the field, but the more timid of the men hung back, and followed very slowly with the women. Had it been merely mortal foes their ruler had called upon them to fight, they would each and all of them have rushed eagerly to the fray; but against their gods!—the spirits of the air and forest, whose vengeance they lived in continual dread of,—against these they could not stand.

Guntra never left her people until the day was at an end, and the whole field reaped; then she went back to the village with a feeling almost of exultation in her heart. She had defied the gods, and conquered; and if she had escaped their fury here, might not her children have done so likewise? and a ray of something like hope crept into her heart with this daring thought.

But the next morning she was startled by seeing one of the younger bards come into the village, for she knew he came as a messenger from the Druids, and she guessed that they had heard and were displeased at the corn being cut.

But the harp was not struck today, although he carried it himself. The message was not to her people, but to herself. She was summoned to appear before the sacred council the following day to receive the commands of the priests and lawgivers of the land. With ready woman-wit Guntra saw that all the corn must be cut today if her people were to be kept from starving during the coming winter months; and so as soon as the bard had left the village, she summoned a council of her warriors, and telling them of the command she had received, bade them assemble the people, and lead them forth to the fields once more to reap the remainder of their crops. It was to be brought home and stored in some empty huts the next day while she was attending the sacred council, for she doubted not that she would receive a command from the Druids forbidding her, or her people to touch the corn since their predictions had failed concerning the Romans.

She had not seen the chief of the council since the departure of Jugurtha and Norma, and she wondered how the old man would receive her. She almost quailed beneath the gaze of those fiery eyes, that looked at her from the hard, stern, set face that never had been known to show pity for man or woman, when at length she reached the oak tree, and stood before the assembled priests and lawgivers.

"Daughter of Britain, know that the gods are offended with thee and thy people," said a bard rising, and speaking in a hard, mechanical voice. "The sacrifice hath been withheld—the sacrifice that was due to them, and our land is given over to the power of the Romans, a people of strange tongue and strange religion."

"But the Romans have not appeared against us for many days," Guntra ventured to say.

"Peace!" thundered the old Druid who ruled the council; "we summoned thee not to hear thy words, but that thou mayest receive our commands. The Romans have not attacked us, therefore we judge they fear our strength and power, and so we will attack them."

Guntra lifted her head proudly. "Your commands shall be obeyed," she said, "and I myself will lead the attack."

"That is well-spoken, daughter of Britain," said the Druid, "thou shalt thyself lead forth the warriors when the round moon hath three times shrunk to a crescent and grown dim."

"Not until three moons have passed away!" exclaimed Guntra in surprise.

"Our command is that three moons rise and set ere thou go forth," said the Druid, sternly.

"Go forth to war in midwinter!" said the lady, as if doubting the evidence of her senses or the sanity of the Druid.

"Even so. The command of the gods is that thou attack the Romans in midwinter, when they think we are all fast asleep or hunting the wolves from our villages."

At the mention of these fierce animals, who often came down in whole packs from the forest and fell upon a village, Guntra shuddered. What would become of the helpless women and children of her people, if these dreadful foes attacked them while she was gone forth with the men against the Roman camp? The thought of what these poor creatures would endure left to fight alone with a pack of wolves, gave her courage to appeal against this command to leave the village unprotected in the winter. But the fierce Druid only frowned as she concluded her appeal.

"Your tribe are indeed weak and pitiful, and unworthy the name of Britons, if the women cannot take target and spear and drive back the wolves from their homes. I tell you it is the command of the gods that your tribe go forth against the Romans, and that ye bring back a train of captives for the sacrifices that shall be offered, when the leaf-buds are bursting on the trees."

Sadly Guntra turned away as she was curtly dismissed by the council. What to do she did not know. Disobey the all-powerful Druids she dare not, and yet how could she lead forth her warriors to wage an uncertain fight against the Romans, when their homes were likely to be desolated by their foes from the forest? Then for themselves, too, they were likely to perish of cold and hunger in the woods, which, affording them food in the summer months, in the winter could offer them nothing but a choice of deaths—either to be lost in the morass; or, weakened by hunger, to fall a victim to the wild boars or wolves.

She had quite forgotten the orders she had given to gather in the crops, in the pressing anxiety of this new difficulty; and when she heard the shout that greeted her approach to the village, her heart almost stood still with expectancy. Surely her children had been found, or had ventured to return to their native village; and she hurried on so rapidly that her guard of honour could scarcely keep up with her.

All too quickly was she undeceived. In a few minutes she understood why the sheaves of corn were being waved so joyously: it had all been cut without a single mishap, and was now being stored in the rude granaries prepared for it. It was almost the only agriculure they had learned as yet, and this they had gained from the invading Romans; and Guntra, as she looked at the golden sheaves, could

RUDE: *crudely built*

almost thank them coming, since they had taught them how to provide food for the winter months; for she could remember tales being told to her, by those who had seen such horrors of whole villages being desolated, because the inhabitants could not gather a sufficiency of acorns, wild fruit, and roots of plants to last them through the winter season.

She checked the sigh that involuntarily arose as she understood the reason of the shouting. Her people had food for their children, and she would be glad in their gladness, although she was a childless widow with none to comfort her, and little in her life to make her wish to live, and nothing beyond this life that she could look forward to as consolation for its trials and sorrows.

She had no hope of ever seeing her dear ones again either in this life or the next, for none could tell whether when the soul passed into the body of a bird or animal, it ever recognized those who had been loved on earth.

But although there was little hope in this life, and none for the next, that she had ever heard of, Guntra resolved to do her duty by her people, and so as soon as she had reached home she summoned a council of her warriors, resolving to abide by their advice rather than the commands of the Druids in the present difficulty; for her faith in them and their predictions had been greatly shaken during the last few weeks.

CHAPTER VIII

A ROMAN SOLDIER

THE news brought by their princess was enough to turn even a British warrior's cheek pale with alarm, but hard and cruel as the command might be, and uncertain as the result must be, they decided that it would be better to risk their wives and little ones being left to the mercy of the wolves, than offend the Druids and their dreaded forest spirits.

So it was settled that at the appointed time they should set forth on their expedition against the Roman camp, headed by Guntra herself in her war chariot, and that in the meanwhile preparations should be made for taking a stock of provisions with them, and the huts should be strengthened to resist the attacks of the wolves. A few spears and javelins were likewise to be left in the village, for women knew how to wield these weapons, and would probably have to use them before the winter was over.

It doubtless disconcerted the Druids not a little to find that the tribe had gathered in their corn without disaster. They had calculated that after their threatening prediction, the people would be afraid to touch it, and so it would lie and rot in the fields, where they would be able to point to it as an evidence of the power and anger of their gods.

But the fields were cleared, and the Britons were industriously strengthening their huts, and putting up firm palisades to keep off the wolves, who had been heard at a distance but as yet had not appeared, so that it seemed likely all the predictions of evil would fail.

Had Guntra followed her own will in the matter, she would have bid defiance to the Druids, and not have gone out against the Romans at this season of the year, but her countrymen shrunk with horror from such disobedience, and declared themselves more ready to encounter death by starvation, or in the morass, than offend the gods and priests further by remaining at home.

So at the appointed time Guntra and her warriors set forth, just as Jugurtha had done a few months before, only then each one's heart had beat high with hope, and many had caught the fiery enthusiasm of their young leader. But there was little hope, and no enthusiasm now. Guntra stood erect in her war chariot, leaning on her spear, looking like some stern offended goddess, but no outward emotion showed the agony she was enduring at that moment. British matrons were not wont to shed useless tears in those days, but many a heart

PALISADES: *fences made of stakes pounded into the ground*
WONT: *in the habit*

died with fear, as they stood at the palisades of the village, and looked across the plain covered with snow, and thought of the swamps and dreary woods that would have to be passed before the Roman camp was reached. To Guntra her warriors were almost as her own children now; and, in taking command of the expedition, she had resolved to secure their safety as far as possible while traveling. She had therefore formed a plan before setting out, which, if it occupied more time, was less dangerous, although it gave the Romans some notice of their approach,—a fact the lady had altogether overlooked in making her calculations. Some of her warriors ventured to tell her that it was not wise to approach so near the camp; but Guntra scorned to go back, and ordered her men to encamp at the edge of the wood, that they might recruit their strength after their long and weary march, before attacking the enemy. But she herself felt no weariness yet. Almost unconsciously to herself she had half-hoped to see something of her children as they came through the woods; and now, this her last hope had faded, she felt weary and sick at heart, but too restless to sit down in her chariot, and so she went forward to look at this famous camp and colony of Londinium.

From where she stood on a little hillock she could see the Great Keep,* where Roman cohorts watched night and day, and where the sentinels could now be seen steadily pacing backwards and

* WHERE THE TOWER OF LONDON NOW STANDS

RECRUIT: *recover*

forwards on the massive ramparts; Guntra's heart grew faint with fear as she looked at these. It was like throwing away the lives of her warriors to attempt an attack against such foes, and she resolved to seek the help of another tribe of her countrymen before commencing hostilities. To her surprise she met one of her warriors as she returned, bringing her the news that other armed Britons with war chariots were approaching the spot, but whether they came to attack *them*, or as their allies against the Romans, they could not tell.

Guntra resolved to ascertain this as soon as possible, and doubted not but that she should prevail upon the chief to turn his arms against the common foe of their country, even if he had come with hostile intentions against herself; but to her surprise and dismay, she heard that nothing could prevent this chief and his followers from attacking her tribe. More than once had they trespassed upon ground that did not belong to them, and now this last insult and menace, as they chose to consider this last act of Guntra's, in marching her warriors through their territory, could not be allowed to go unpunished.

No wonder the Romans gained such power in the land, when the rightful owners fell out and fought about such trifles. It must have afforded the cohorts of Rome no small amusement and pleasure to see the foes, whom they thought were coming against them with united force, divide

COHORTS: *divisions of about 500 soldiers*
ASCERTAIN: *make certain of*

and fight a fierce battle within sight of their own ramparts.

Guntra in her war chariot led on her men to resist the attack of their neighbours, for she would not strike the first blow against her native countrymen, and her clansmen had little relish for this kind of warfare, when they had come out with the express determination of fighting their foes the Romans. But they fought bravely and well, until they saw their leader sink down in her chariot pierced with an arrow. Then they fell into confusion and disorder, and many were taken prisoners.

But the triumph of their enemies was of short duration, for scarcely was the battle over before Roman trumpets were heard close at hand, and soon a cohort of legionaries were seen approaching. Both parties of Britons turned to face the enemy, and greeted them with a shower of arrows that struck down one tall centurion and several of his men, but hindered not the onward march of the rest, who quickly filled up the ranks of their fallen companions.

The Britons with a shout rushed forward, pell-mell, with headlong fury, against that advancing wall of shields and spears, and for a moment Roman discipline was checked in its onward march by British heroism and bravery. But only for a moment. Like the resistless waves of the sea those eagle crests came on, beating back their undisciplined foes, who, weakened by the recent strife

LEGIONARIES: *Roman soldiers*

among themselves, soon gave way and were driven at the spear's point to take refuge in the wood. Many were wounded and taken prisoners, and among them the unfortunate Guntra. She had fallen down in her chariot insensible, and remained so during the whole time the battle was raging between the Romans and her own people, so that she knew nothing of what was going on, until the jolting of the chariot made her sensible of increasing agony; and then opening her eyes she saw to her dismay that she was surrounded by dark-visaged men, whose eagle crests proclaimed them to be Romans.

With a slight scream and a shudder of horror, Guntra thought of her position; she was a prisoner —a slave. She, a high-born British princess, might have to call one of these soldiers her master, and she sank down in the chariot, hoping she might never open her eyes or see the light of day again. There was great rejoicing throughout the Roman camp at the complete rout of the Britons, and nearly a shipload of prisoners were dispatched to the coast, to await the sailing of the first galley for the opposite shore. Marcinius had been engaged in the fray—had been compelled to take command of one company, for his centurion was one of the first to be struck down by the arrows of the Britons, and Marcinius had to rally his men and take his place. He had done it simply as a matter of duty as a Roman soldier; but the prætor in command

INSENSIBLE: *unconscious*
DARK-VISAGED: *dark-faced*

had noticed the action, and when he heard that the centurion was dead he took care Marcinius should succeed him.

It was a promotion not at all expected, and scarcely desired, although the increased pay he would receive from the Emperor would solve one or two domestic problems that just now were puzzling him, the most puzzling of which was what was to be done with his two British slaves. There would be little difficulty about this, now he could help them both. Norma could be taught to wait on his wife and daughter, and Jugurtha could clean his armour, and do the various kinds of work needful in the house.

The young Briton was rapidly gaining strength now, and often had an opportunity of seeing how his fellow-countrymen were treated by their Roman masters—treatment which strongly contrasted with his own position in the household of Marcinius, but which he now began to understand resulted from the difference of religious faith. Most of these conquerors of his land worshipped Jupiter and Apollo; but whatever refinement there might be about the worship of these deities, as compared with his own Druidical superstition, there was little difference in the way in which they treated their slaves. Only these Christians seemed to understand what kindness meant, and Jugurtha could appreciate it as shown to his little sister, and in a lesser degree as shown to himself. Had he

fallen into any other hands than those of Marcinius, he would have been left to perish, he knew;
and if life was not of much value to him for his
own sake, it was for his sister's, so that he could
feel grateful to the Roman for sheltering him, and
nursing him during his illness.

But the news that the Britons were gathering
their forces again to make another attack upon
London roused all his fiery spirit, and he chafed
at the bonds that held him inactive, and probably
would have tried to escape and join his countrymen outside the walls, but for the thought that
this might bring suffering upon Norma; and then
his own remaining weakness rendered it uncertain whether he would be of much service to his
friends, even if he made good his escape. Marcinius saw the restlessness of his slave, and deeply as
he might feel for him he knew that the kindest
thing was to keep him close in the house, where
he could hear little, and see less, of what was going
on beyond the walls.

So Jugurtha did not know that it was his own
tribe, led by his noble mother, who were so close
at hand, and not until the battle was over, and the
prisoners being brought in, did he hear of the first
fight between those who should have united all
their strength against the invader of their country. When he did hear of this he breathed hard for
a minute or two, and then said through his teeth,
"Their defeat was merited, Roman. All other

quarrels should be forgotten between Britons, now that they seek to rid themselves of a foreign foe."

But Marcinius shook his head, and said, sadly, "It is not so easy to forget a quarrel or forgive a wrong."

Jugurtha stared, and then his face flushed crimson. "Do you remember the day I saw you first—when I met you in the wood, and called you a Roman dog?" he said, quickly.

"Yes, I recognized you again soon after I had taken you prisoner," said Marcinius.

"I knew it," replied Jugurtha; "and yet you never taunted me for that, or the words I spoke the day you brought me here. Roman, you must find it easy to forgive!"

But the soldier replied, "You know not the haughty pride of us Romans, or you would not speak thus. It is not I, Marcinius, the soldier of the Emperor, who could forgive, but the grace of the Lord Jesus Christ in me. Marcinius the Christian can forgive, because his Lord and Master has forgiven him, and bid him love all men even as himself."

"And this is what your religion teaches you. Truly it is a strange religion," said Jugurtha, "but I would fain learn it; for if it made all men tender and patient as thou art, Marcinius, there would be less sorrow and suffering in the world."

It was the first time the young Briton had spoken of this, since the day it had been first introduced

FAIN: *gladly*

to his notice. The little meetings for Christian worship had been held every day in the *atrium*, but Jugurtha had expressed no wish to be present, and Marcinius would not force even his slave to take part in a worship that must come from the heart, and spring from love to God, if it were true service. He was willing to wait and pray, that the Spirit of God should first touch that fierce proud heart; and now his prayers were answered, for Jugurtha was anxious to learn more of the truth as it is in Jesus. Perhaps the childish talk of his little sister made Jugurtha more anxious to become acquainted with this new strange faith; for Norma often now spoke of the Saviour who loved her, and whom she was going to see one day. Her brother began to think there must be some truth in this faith, for the child had no doubt about the happy home being prepared for her beyond the stars, and often spake as though God was very near to her.

Unconsciously the fierce, proud spirit of the young Briton was learning to venerate gentleness, goodness, and truth, instead of cruelty, passion, and power; and thus his heart was being prepared by God's Spirit for the reception of the truth. But it was hard to make Jugurtha understand the necessity of Christ's death, and to induce him to believe that He could have loved man so much as to suffer this for him, until Marcinius suddenly asked, "Would not you brave death for the sake of your sister?"

VENERATE: *honor, respect*

"Did I not do it when I rescued her from the Druids?" said Jugurtha, quickly; and he gave Marcinius a fuller account than he had previously done of the rescue of little Norma, and his flight to the woods.

"And your sister knew not the danger she was in; but you did not wait for that to snatch her from your cruel priests," said Marcinius. "So it is with the Lord Christ, and the salvation He offers us. He saw that we were in danger, in the power of sin and Satan, and He snatched us away, saying, 'Go and sin no more;'[1] but though He saved us, He had to yield His own life a ransom for ours; He had to take our place, that we might go free."

"And He could love me like that—as much as I love Norma!" said Jugurtha, wonderingly. "Nay, but I thought this love that I bore to my mother and sister was a weakness, and yet your God can love too."

"Our 'God is love,'" said Marcinius, reverently; "He would have us think of Him and call Him 'our Father;'[2] He loves you as tenderly as you can love your sister, and asks you to believe this, and love all men for His sake."

"It is strange—passing strange," said Jugurtha, musingly; but in a minute or two he added, more sadly, "This religion cannot be for Britons—it can never be the religion of Britain."

"Nay, I do not despair even of this," said Marcinius; "although I may not see it, God can do it; and

---

[1] JOHN 8:11   [2] MATTHEW 6:9

I pray for your island as I do for my Rome, that God will make His truth to conquer. What Britons have accepted Britons may yet accept; and two of your countrymen in our camp here have learned to love and trust in the Lord Jesus Christ as their Saviour."

"And my little sister has likewise learned to know and love this God, whom she calls the Saviour. Roman, I owe you much that you have made my sister happy; for she has ceased to fret so sorely for her mother since she learned your religion."

"Not that she has forgotten her," said Marcinius, quickly; "I would not have the child forget her mother, but my Valeria has taught her to pray for her now, and she believes the great God will take care of her mother, and teach her to know His love by and by."

Jugurtha shook his head. "That can never be," he said; "we hear nought of your religion in our village, and my mother would never forsake the gods of Britain;" and he heaved a deep sigh as he spoke, for he thought if she could but hear the glad tidings this Roman soldier had to tell, she would be comforted for the loss of her children. He knew how sorely she must have grieved for them both, but he knew not how near she was to them at that very moment.

CHAPTER IX

THE BRITISH SLAVE

THE war chariot with the prostrate figure of Guntra was driven to where the golden eagles of Rome shone most resplendently from helmet and ensign—the Prætorium, where tribunes and centurions were gathered to learn the further commands of their general.

The scythes had been broken from the axletrees of the chariot, but the centurions moved aside as it came near, and left a space for it before the Prætor.

"A British princess, by the helmet of Cæsar!" said the Roman general as he saw the long white robe, and noticed the gold bracelets on her wrists and ankles.

"One of the rebels," said a tall centurion, "and as unconquerable in her hatred as the rest of her race, I doubt not, although she is a woman."

"Ye have done well, my men, to bring this prisoner to me," said the general; "for if this British favourite of our Emperor, the Princess Claudia, who hath married the Roman soldier Pudens, returns

PROSTRATE: *lying flat*
TRIBUNES: *officers commanding legions*

to Britain in the spring, as it is supposed, she will doubtless be glad of a slave, who can tell her somewhat of her native land, as well as prepare the unguents and perfumes for her bath."

"Then thou wilt have her taken good care of?" said a tribune, looking with some pity on the fair blood-stained hair of the lady.

"Yes; she hath been wounded in this fray, let her wounds be carefully dressed as soon as may be, and she can lodge in my house for the present."

Such consideration was not to be shown to the other prisoners. A few whose wounds were very severe, were killed out of hand at once—they were almost envied by their companions, who, weary, wounded and footsore, were driven in groups along the streets of Londinium, to languish in prison until they were carried to Rome.

Guntra's first thought when she awoke from this second fainting fit was for her warriors; but strange faces were around her, and it was a strange language she heard whispered by the side of her couch. As the property of a great man she would be well-cared-for, and the room in which she was lying was fitted up with every luxury, but the sight of these things only filled the lady's mind with a vague terror, for she knew it must be a Roman house in which she was lying, and that she was no longer free.

She tried to raise herself as she looked round, but she was weak from loss of blood, and the pain

UNGUENTS: *ointments*
LANGUISH: *suffer neglect*

in her arm was so severe that she fell back upon
the pile of cushions with a deep groan. In a moment, someone was beside her speaking in sooth-
ing tones, although in a strange language, and
pressing her to take some wine from a cup which
she held to her lips. Guntra drank a little to please
the woman, and then asked about her countrymen—her warriors who had been taken prisoners
with her. But the dark-eyed woman only shook her
head, and turned to her work of weaving a chaplet
of exotic flowers for her favourite goddess, Flora.
She could not understand what this British captive
said, but she resolved to learn her language, that
she might teach her to worship the gods of Rome,
and then they could go together to the temple of
Diana; for the impulsive girl had taken a great liking to the fair-haired slave.

Guntra lay and watched the nimble fingers twist-
ing leaves and blossoms into a flower-crown. Many
of these the British matron had never seen before;
they were unlike any that grew in her native woods,
and she stretched out her hands to touch them,
and assure herself they were real. The girl smiled
and laid the wreath in the invalid's hand. She
too was a slave, but she never remembered being
otherwise, and she was inclined to take things
lightly, and not trouble herself with too much
thought about anything.

She was pleased that her charge had taken notice of her work. "It is for Flora, who is our goddess

CHAPLET: *wreath*

of flowers," she said, forgetting that Guntra could not understand her language. But she thought of it immediately afterwards, and opening the door leading into the *atrium*, she took her wreath, and placing it on the head of the statue just opposite, she clasped her hands and kneeled down. The lady understood her then. It was an offering for her god, but she did not wish to hear more about it; her mind was too full of anxious forebodings concerning her warriors and her people to give much heed to anything else.

But her young nurse was determined she should know how far superior the gods of Rome were to those of Britain; and she began to make inquiries among her fellow-slaves in the neighbourhood, as to where she could learn this barbarous language. She did not have to wait long for information. She soon heard that the new centurion, Marcinius, understood the language of the barbarians, and that he sometimes read from a roll of parchment, and translated it from the Latin to the British tongue as he read, that one or two slaves who went to hear the reading might understand it.

"Then I will go with them, if I can find out at what hour this roll is to be read," said the girl. "Is it of our great god, Jupiter, he reads?" she asked.

"Nay, I cannot tell; I trouble not myself with these things," replied her companion. "They say this Marcinius differs from most of our soldiers in that he is kind to friend and foe alike, and will turn none from his doors who desire to hear his reading."

"Of which he is mightily vain, I doubt not," said the other, pertly. Doubtless she thought it would gratify his vanity to see a woman come in with the few soldiers and slaves who gathered in the humble *atrium* each day; and Marcinius certainly did feel some surprise when he saw her enter; but it was thankfulness that another desired to hear the word of life, rather than vanity; that made him raise his voice as he read, so that she might hear distinctly from her corner near the door.

Each day she came at the appointed hour, creeping in after all the rest, and slipping out again before any of the others stirred from their places, so that no one had an opportunity of speaking to her, even if they had felt so disposed. She was learning by this means and the help she received from Guntra at home, to understand the barbarian language; but it was not all she learned. For some time she paid little attention to anything but the translation, caring nothing for the subject of the reading; but by degrees she became interested in this, and the strange, glad news it brought of another God, more powerful than Jupiter, who loved all men, and was more beneficent even than her favourite goddess, Flora.

But this did not deter her from trying to interest the British matron in her favourite deity. If there was another god to be added to the

BENEFICENT: *good and kind*

already crowded Pantheon, they would receive
news of it shortly from Rome; and so she went to
listen to the reading of Marcinius, attended the
temple of Diana, standing in the midst of the city,
and made flower-crowns for Flora, and tried to
make Guntra believe in her beneficence—efforts
which the lady received kindly, but took little
heed of.

What were flowers to her now, a captive in the
hands of her enemies? Their very beauty and per-
fume only reminded her of her bonds, and made
her sigh for the free upland breeze of her native
hills, and the rustle of the oak leaves in her own
forests. Legends of the prowess of Jupiter, the su-
preme deity of Rome, could not gladden her heart,
for it must be by the power of this god the Romans
had crushed her people, and therefore the gods of
Rome could never be the gods of Britain.

So the good-natured slave, who had been appointed first to act as her nurse, and then to teach
her how to prepare the perfumes and unguents
for a Roman bath, found her charge less willing
to learn than she had anticipated, and not at all
anxious to accompany her to the magnificent temple of Diana. Indeed, this British captive showed
little taste for Roman refinement and luxury, either in the mode of living, or the outward adorn-
ment of houses and temples. Art had little charm
for her, and she longed for her rude homely hut;
for her couch of dried leaves and wolfskins was far

PANTHEON: *the temple for all of the accepted Roman gods*

preferable to the cushions and shawls upon which she now reposed.

The Roman general was pleased to find his noble captive so fully recovered from her wounds, and ordered that every pains should be taken to instruct her in the duties of a Roman waiting-maid; for he doubted not that the princess Claudia would be gratified at receiving such a present from his hands, and he was anxious through her to win the favour of her husband Pudens. So Guntra had little to complain of in her outward condition just now, except that the endless mixing of perfumes wearied her; and thinking of her children or her warriors, she would forget what she was about, and often the whole compound was spoiled. These mistakes caused little beyond a burst of laughter among her fellow-slaves and instructors at first; but after a time they began to lose their patience, and even complained of the waste this caused,—not that they cared about their master's property being used extravagantly—extravagance was the ruling principle of a Roman household in those days,—but because they were growing tired of teaching one who seemed so stupid at learning what every Roman girl seemed to know intuitively.

At last, the Roman general was himself spoken to upon the subject. Those who understood such matters declared that the captive would never make a serviceable waiting-maid, and it was useless

REPOSED: *lay*

to try to teach her any longer. The Prætor was greatly annoyed when he heard this account. To his idea all women were alike; and why Guntra should not learn all the requirements of a civilized toilette he could not tell: he thought all women took to such things naturally; and so he decided it was the native obstinacy of her character that prevented her from learning these things.

It was the more vexatious just now, as the spring was opening, and Claudia and her husband would shortly arrive from Rome; and thinking of this, the Prætor grew so angry, that turning to one of his attendants who stood near, he ordered him to fetch the British matron to his presence.

In a few minutes Guntra came in, still wearing the long white robe as in the days when she was free, and looking as fearlessly at her master now as she would have done had he merely come to her native village to drive off the flocks and herds of her tribe. She looked as little like a docile waiting-woman as it was possible to conceive, and the Roman general, as he looked at her, thought so too.

"So you refuse to learn the duties of your office," he said, bending a stern look upon her.

"The duties of my office are those of a chief over a tribe of Britons," replied Guntra, proudly, "and from these you have taken me, and hold me here a captive."

"But you rebelled against the Roman power and authority," said the general.

TOILETTE: *grooming and dressing*

"I owned not your authority," replied Guntra, "nor will my people ever own it."

"By the helmet of Cæsar, then, you shall feel our power," said the general, angrily.

"I have already felt it—am made to feel it every day of my life," said Guntra, bitterly.

"What? you complain of the treatment you have received while under my roof—you, a barbarian slave!"

"Nay, but I am a free-born Briton," said Guntra, proudly.

"I say you are a slave—my slave, and your nation is the vassal of Rome."

Guntra raised her hand, and her eyes flashed with scorn and anger. "*I* may be enslaved," she said, "but my nation—my proud, brave Britain—will never bow to the eagles of Rome."

"Peace, woman, and begone!" shouted the general in his anger, for he knew that Guntra was only speaking the sentiments of every tribe of her people, and that they were like herself—the most unconquerable nation the Roman arms had ever waged war against. But Guntra would not be thus summarily dismissed; she had something more to say to the Roman general; and so, folding her arms calmly in front, she hurled menaces and defiance against all the Roman power in the land.

The Prætor was fairly surprised into calmness while she was speaking, but his anger broke forth

OWNED: *acknowledged*
VASSAL: *servant*
SUMMARILY: *quickly*

with redoubled fury as she concluded her angry speech.

"You have not known what it is to be a slave yet!" he said. "But you shall know it ere long. Ho, Hippias!" he called; "here, take this woman to the slave prison at once, and tell them to sell her to anyone who will give two hundred sesterces for her. Some of my men may like a British scullion," he added, "and I shall wish them joy of their bargain."

The rough soldier would have drawn near to take Guntra by the arm, but she ordered him to keep at a distance with a gesture as haughty as any Roman patrician dame might have done; and with a last menacing look at the Prætor, she walked slowly out, followed by the soldier.

It was the first time Guntra had been into the streets of London. She had shrunk from looking upon the trophies of Roman art and conquest that would everywhere meet her view here, for to her they only spoke of the enslavement of her people, and of the power of the oppressor; and even now she would fain have closed her eyes and shut out the sight of all the grandeur; but this was impossible, and unconsciously she stood in speechless surprise, when they reached the temple of Diana, with its elegant columns and massive pillars.

The guard of soldiers surrounding her allowed her to remain for a moment to gaze at the building, for they were half-awed by her calm dignity, and more than half-afraid of rousing her anger; so

HALF-AWED: *half-overwhelmed*

Guntra gazed as long as she pleased at the temple of the goddess, and then turned to look at a colossal statue of Jupiter, and while she was looking at this, a group of British slaves passed. All the Britons seen in Londinium were slaves, so that it needed not the distinctive mark of having the head uncovered to announce this fact, and yet the soldiers around her touched their helmets with something of pride as they looked after her countrymen, whom they had deprived of their most dearly cherished right—freedom.

Guntra turned to look too, wondering whether any of these were of her tribe. She started and clasped her hands as her eyes fell upon one—the tallest and youngest of the group, and she would have run after him down the straight road that led to the Great Keep, had not her guards held her back.

"Let me go—let me go," she panted,—"it is my son—my Jugurtha. I must speak to him once more!" she added.

But she might as well have spoken to the winds. Her guard was inexorable: possibly they did not understand a word she was saying, for she spoke in her own language, and few of the Roman soldiers understood the dialect of the islanders; but even if they had understood her appeal, they dared not heed it more than to give a few compassionate words, for the commands of the general had been that she should be strictly guarded, and

INEXORABLE: *unyielding*

not allowed to speak to anyone on her way to the prison—or rather, slave warehouse. So paying little attention to the passionate words she spoke, the soldiers hurried her on as fast as they could, vexed at her having seen any of her countrymen, for she was attracting the attention of those they met in the street, and by and by the Prætor might hear of their lax discipline in allowing her to stay a moment to look at the temple.

The idea that it was her son had taken full possession of Guntra's mind now and for a moment she forgot his condition, in the joy she felt at knowing he was still alive; but when her guards refused to let her go after him, then the full horror of her position, and his too, seemed to dawn upon her for the first time. She was a slave—in cruel bondage to another; not even to speak to her own son could she break through the power of those who held her, and for awhile the thought of this almost froze her soul, and she followed her guards almost mechanically.

But when at last the gloomy, desolate-looking prison was reached, Guntra refused to enter; she would stay outside, she said, and wait for her son to pass; and it was only by main force that she was taken inside the door and placed in charge of the keeper. Once inside, and all hope of seeing Jugurtha at an end, the lady fell with a deep groan to the ground, and unconsciousness for a time relieved her mind of its load of anguish.

LAX: *careless*
MAIN: *utmost*

CHAPTER X

MOTHER AND SON

JUGURTHA had not noticed the group of Roman soldiers standing near the temple of their deity. They were to be met with at every point here in Londinium; and the young Briton had little love for the conquerors, and less desire to gaze upon the hated eagles that had swooped down upon his native land, and held it fast in cruel bondage; so that he paid little heed to the imperial legionaries whom he met in the streets. One or two of his companions, however, who were growing more accustomed to their new mode of life, had noticed that a woman was the center of the group, and they spoke of this to Jugurtha; but he only clenched his hands and set his teeth hard as he walked on more resolutely, for he knew all too well that he was powerless to help a countrywoman, however great might be her wrongs.

As they drew near the quarters of the soldiers, however, the slaves noticed the Roman girl who had so often attended their religious meetings of late; and one more curious than the rest stopped and asked her reason for coming there.

The girl looked confused at the direct question, and stammered out something about wanting to learn the "barbarians' language," but then added quickly,—

"I shall not have to come again, for my master has sent her away;" and tears of compassion filled her eyes as she spoke.

"Who is sent away?" asked one.

"The British woman who was a captive in our house. She was proud and obstinate, like the rest of her race, and would not learn the duties of a Roman waiting-maid, but was ever talking of her warriors, and how bravely they had fought against our soldiers."

"And they would force a British maiden, who had led warriors to the battle, to learn the weak and childish arts of a bower-woman!" exclaimed Jugurtha, fiercely.

The girl looked up as he spoke.

"By our sweet goddess Flora, thou art like this captive woman!" she said.

The young Briton started and turned pale as he said, eagerly,—

"I am like this captive? Tell me, did she wear a white robe; and bracelets of gold on her arms and ankles?" he asked.

"Nay, I saw not aught of jewels," replied the girl; "but that is not to be wondered at, seeing our

soldiers brought her in sorely wounded from an
arrow. Doubtless they robbed her," she added,
darting a piercing look at a tall legionary who was
standing near.

The man smiled, but did not reply; and Jugurtha
pushed him aside in his eagerness to hear more
concerning this stranger.

"Was she tall?" he asked.

"Yes, almost as tall as thou art, and lofty in her
ways as our noblest Roman dames."

"Britons are nobler than Roman robbers," exclaimed Jugurtha, "and my mother is the noblest
matron of them all. If it is she who has fallen into
your power, she will not quickly learn your ways.
Tell me, girl, was her robe of white wool, reaching
from her shoulders to her feet?" he said.

The girl nodded, and said,—

"I never saw her in aught else, for she broke into
fierce anger when I asked her to wear Roman gar-
ments, and would have nothing but this same old
white robe."

"It is my mother, I doubt not!" exclaimed
Jugurtha. "Girl, where is she now? Take me to her
at once," he said, passionately.

But the girl drew back in some alarm.

"Oh, these dreadful savage Britons!" she said,
with an affected toss of the head.

Jugurtha was in no mood for affectation just
now, and seized her by the wrist.

"Do you hear me, girl? It is my mother whom
you hold captive. Take me to her at once."

AFFECTED: *exaggerated*

She was fairly frightened now, and uttered a scream as she said,—

"I can't! I can't! she has gone to be sold."

Jugurtha dropped her hand, and staggered backwards at those words.

"Gone to be sold!" he repeated. "My noble mother a common slave!" and he covered his face with his hands to hide the emotion he could not subdue.

Hard as their own lot was, his companions could not but feel touched at the sight of Jugurtha's sorrow, and as he hastened away to hide his grief, they went to their tried friend, his master, and told him all that they had heard.

Marcinius was both grieved and surprised to hear of the treatment Guntra had received from the Prætor. He believed Jugurtha's story; and if this was his mother who had been captured before the walls of London, she had a right to expect better treatment from her captors. This British princess, who was almost daily expected to return to her native land, had been treated with all honour and courtesy by their Emperor Claudius, after whom she was named. True, she had married a Roman general now, and as the wife of Pudens would be entitled to the same respect as a Roman matron, but this had been accorded to her before, when she was one of "Cæsar's household."

Other reports had reached him, too, concerning Claudia's residence at Rome. He had heard that she had attended the preaching and teaching

TRIED: *proven*

of a Jewish prisoner who had appealed to Cæsar; and, like so many others waiting for tardy justice, had been kept nearly two years in suspense, but not in idleness. The very doctrine his countrymen accused him of teaching in Judea, he taught now in Rome, and Marcinius believed it was the same he had learned from the old Jewish fisherman at Joppa. If this was so, and Claudia was among the "saints of Cæsar's household," brighter days might be in store for this dark, cruel, superstitious land of Britain; for she, like all who had learned to know that "God is love," and Christ had died to redeem all men, would be anxious that others should learn the same truth.

And for Rome, too, there was hope dawning at last; and if only this proud imperial city—this mistress of nations—would embrace the gospel, what a blessing might Rome become to the world!

So thought and so mused this Roman centurion, until he was interrupted by the entrance of his British slave, upon whom the chains of slavery pressed so lightly that he often forgot he owned a Roman master. But it seemed that he had not forgotten it today, for as he came into the *atrium* he said hastily,—

"Marcinius, you have ever been kind to me, and I owe you a debt of gratitude I can never repay; but the Lord Christ, whom you have taught me to love, will reward you for all, even for this last favour I am about to ask."

TARDY: *slow-moving*

"What is it, Jugurtha?" asked his master, kindly, seeing he stopped, as if half-afraid he should meet with a refusal.

"Will you sell me, Master?" asked Jugurtha.

Marcinius started and looked grieved.

"Sell you, Jugurtha?" he repeated; "are you not satisfied with your service to me?"

"Satisfied as I could ever be with slavery I am," said Jugurtha; "but still I ask you to sell me, though my lot may be ten times harder, and I may be sent to fight in your circus at Rome."

"But why do you wish this?" asked Marcinius.

A look of agony crossed Jugurtha's face.

"My mother is a slave," he said, "and I would redeem her. Here with our Norma she could learn from her lips the faith that conquers death, and with you, would forget her bonds as much as she could anywhere; but if she is sold from the prison, who can tell what she will suffer, or whether she will ever hear of that love that was greater than any we can know?"

But Marcinius still looked troubled.

"Are you sure this captive is your mother?" he asked.

"Yes," replied Jugurtha. "I have been to the slave prison and looked on her face, but she was unconscious of my presence; and I cannot see her again until I take her place."

"But what is the price asked for her?" inquired Marcinius.

The proud young Briton winced at the question, necessary though it was.

"I have not asked," he said, sadly, "but I should think my strength would be taken by any in exchange for hers;" and he held forth his bare stalwart arm in proof of his ability to work.

"Doubtless more sesterces would be given for you than for your mother," said Marcinius; "but have you thought that I shall lose your services in cleaning my armour and performing various other duties for me, and gain but an encumbrance with another woman in the house?"

Jugurtha's face fell.

"True," he said; "I had forgotten. O Roman, how accursed is your slavery! for I cannot even save my mother when I would."

"Nay, I said not that," replied Marcinius. "I know that this slavery is a curse; and sometimes I know not whether I ought to hold you and your sister in bonds, when the Lord Christ hath made you free, but—"

"Nay, nay, talk not of Norma now; it is of my mother I would speak," interrupted Jugurtha. "Tell me how I can save my mother," he added, impatiently.

It was a puzzling question for the soldier to answer. From all he had heard, this proud British matron had offended the general, and to make any stir on her behalf might be taken as a dire insult by him. Thus thought the Roman centurion,

ENCUMBRANCE: *burden*

but Marcinius the Christian argued that this poor oppressed woman was one for whom his Lord had died, and therefore he ought to make some effort on her behalf, as well as for the sake of Jugurtha, whom he had begun to love as a brother in the faith.

But it would be necessary to proceed with caution in this matter, he could see, and the first thing to be ascertained was the price for which Guntra was to be sold. This he heard sooner than he expected, for one of the guards sent with her mentioned the price his master had fixed as her value.

"Two hundred sesterces!" repeated Marcinius, when the sum was named. "The woman cannot be worth much to fetch no more than that."

"You forget she is old, and obstinate withal," said one; "I doubt whether the Prætor will get even that for her."

"It is not a large sum to give for a slave, but more than I possess," debated Marcinius. "If I were to sell Jugurtha, he would fetch five hundred at least; but it is long since I sold a man, and I like not such traffic now."

The young Briton, in his impatience, thought his master almost cruel when he went to his duty on the ramparts, without saying a word concerning his mother, and in the first moments of anger at this, he felt strongly tempted to go and offer himself to the keeper of the prison in exchange for her. But the new principles he had learned with this religion of love forbade his taking this step. He was the property of another; not only by right of being his master, but there was a closer bond still—gratitude and love, and these forbade him to throw himself into the hands of the prison keeper without his benefactor's permission.

Marcinius, however, had not forgotten his slave's anxieties. While going his rounds of the Great Keep, and looking across towards the forests and plains of Britain, he was revolving in his mind various plans for raising the necessary sum to purchase Guntra, none of which seemed practicable but the one suggested by Jugurtha himself—that he should be sold.

How much the war-worn Roman had learned to love the young Briton he did not know until now that he seemed called upon to part with him. Various plans that he had formed too, for getting him installed in the household of Claudia must come to nought now, for the centurion as well as the general had hoped much from the visit of this British princess to the camp; only the hopes of one were centered entirely in himself, while the other sought not his own advancement, but the benefit of his slave.

It was with some reluctance Marcinius told his wife of his resolve to part with Jugurtha, and bid her prepare the two girls for the parting. Jugurtha himself had received the news with an

PRACTICABLE: *possible to use*

exclamation of delight, that was quickly followed
by a burst of passionate grief as he recalled all
the kindness he had received from Marcinius. He
knew too, that his master was sacrificing much for
the sake of helping him, and that endeared him
the more, and he hoped his mother would not
disdain to clean a Roman centurion's armour, although she might refuse to learn the duties of a
waiting-woman.

The parting with Norma was the most bitter moment of all to the young Briton. The little girl positively refused to believe he was not coming back to
her. "No, no," she said, "I have prayed to the great
God and the kind Saviour, and He will bring you
back again just as He has brought Mother."

It seemed at first that the child's prayers would
be answered in a way least anticipated or desired. When Marcinius reached the prison with
Jugurtha, he heard that the captive brought the
day before was very ill, and that her owner, the
Prætor, refused to incur any expense in trying to
cure her.

The young Briton's eyes flashed angrily when
he heard the cruel words, but Marcinius laid his
hand upon him restrainingly while he spoke to
the keeper. "Can we see the woman?" he said, in
a tone of assumed indifference. Without replying,
the man led the way to a long low-arched room,
where on the brick floor on which were scattered
a few dried leaves lay the noble British matron.

Perhaps in her hut at home, the accommoda-
tion would not have been much better, but there
would have been some alleviation to her suffering,
some kindly hand to raise her head, and give her
a draught of water, or some decoction of herbs to
cool her parched lips.

Jugurtha rushed to her side, and pressed his
lips on her burning brow, but there was no smile
of recognition in her heavy eyes; she only raised
her head with a faint moan, and opened her blackened lips as if suffering from intense thirst.

Marcinius, who had followed him, turned and
asked the keeper for some water, at the same time
hinting that he should like him to take a draught
from a wineskin at his expense presently, which
wonderfully facilitated the bringing of the water.
The soldier had learned to deal with sickness in
his various campaigns, and knew that Guntra was
in the first stage of fever, and cooling drink was
what she most needed now.

But it greatly complicated matters to find her
thus; for to sell Jugurtha on the chance of her re-
covery was not to be thought of; at the same time
she must not be left here to perish for want of attention. To bribe the keeper to let him attend to Guntra's wants seemed the only plan he could adopt,
and this he found was not very difficult, more especially when he told the man that Jugurtha could
be trusted to look after his charge if he wished to
leave the place at any time while he was there. By

JUGURTHA'S VISIT TO HIS MOTHER

this means he obtained permission for Jugurtha to visit his mother as often as he liked—a permission the young Briton was ready to thank him for almost on bended knees.

While Marcinius went with the keeper to taste a draught from a wineskin, Jugurtha bathed his mother's throbbing temples, gathered the scattered leaves into a heap to raise her head, and placed her more comfortably on her rude couch. It was hard to leave her when at length Marcinius returned with the keeper, and said they must go back; but the man promised to supply her with water until they returned again; and Marcinius was anxious to get home and consult his wife about preparing some more suitable food than Guntra was likely to get at the prison, as well as some decoction of roots and herbs, considered very efficacious then in such cases.

There seemed an unusual stir in the streets when they left the prison; and Marcinius was somewhat anxious lest there had been another sudden outbreak among the islanders, when he noticed that the people were all hurrying in one direction—towards the Great Keep. But his anxieties were soon set at rest on this account by hearing that a horseman had just arrived from Dover, bringing news that the Imperial galleys conveying the Princess Claudia back to her native land, had left the opposite shore of Gaul, and therefore she might be expected in Londinium within a week.

EFFICACIOUS: *effective*

The news had spread rapidly through the camp and colony, and the gay people, glad of any excuse for a holiday, were hurrying to know what preparations the Prefect would have them make, for the reception of the lady who had been so greatly honoured by the Emperor. Marcinius felt relieved when he heard the news, and somewhat disappointed too, for it would be useless to make any effort on behalf of Jugurtha now; and by the time Guntra was better, Claudia might have left Londinium.

But it was useless to repine at the arrangements of Providence, though doubtless Marcinius thought he could have managed these things better himself, as we often do in our blindness and folly; so he tried to speak cheerfully and hopefully to his slave, as they walked together through the streets, back to the soldiers' quarter of the town.

GAY: *light-hearted*
REPINE: *long for something different*
PROVIDENCE: *God*

CHAPTER XI

THE DISTURBANCE

THE Prætor seemed to have forgotten the British captive when once she was out of the house, for after saying he would be at no further expense for her, and the keeper might do as he pleased with her if she were ill, he never even troubled to inquire whether she were likely to recover or not. Two hundred sesterces was too small a sum for him to trouble himself about, and as the object for which he had secured her had failed, something else must be provided as a present to Claudia instead.

Meanwhile preparations were being made on all sides for the reception of the lady and her numerous train; and various reports were afloat as to the particular temple she would most favour,— that of Diana standing in the midst of Londinium, or that of Apollo* in the adjacent island formed by the winding of the river. Special sacrifices were prepared to be offered at both places in anticipation of the lady's choice, and Marcinius wondered

* WHERE WESTMINSTER ABBEY NOW STANDS

whether she would have the courage to risk offend-
ing all the Roman prejudices, and declare herself
one of the despised Christians.

Jugurtha had expressed some interest in the
talked of return of this princess, although he knew
nothing of his master's plans concerning him; but
now that the day of her arrival was actually fixed,
he took little or no interest in it, for his mind was
almost wholly occupied with his mother.

She lay dangerously ill at the slave prison, and
but for the kindness of Marcinius and his wife,
and the unremitting attentions of Jugurtha, she
must have sunk under the violence of the fever.
But at last, to the great joy of her son, the delirium
left her, and one day, after watching her through a
long sleep, he saw that as she opened her eyes he
was recognized.

"My son—my Jugurtha!" gasped Guntra, trying
to rouse herself as she spoke.

But Jugurtha gently laid her back on the pillow.
"Mother, Mother," was all he could say for a minute
or two, for tears of gladness choked his utterance.

"Where are we?" asked the invalid, trying to
look round her as she spoke.

Her faithful nurse dreaded the sight of those
Roman walls for her, and anxiously bent over her
so as to hide them as much as possible. "Never
mind, Mother, where you are; the great God is
here, and has been very good to us."

"The great God," repeated Guntra, wonderingly.

"Yes, Mother, the God who sent me here to you," said Jugurtha.

"He sent you to me—you, my son, whom I never thought to see again? then there is a good God somewhere, good and kind, instead of fierce and cruel like our forest spirits. Jugurtha, tell me about Him," she added, quickly.

But at this moment Marcinius entered, and whispering to Jugurtha, bade him give her some nourishment, and let her go to sleep again; but while the invalid was taking this, she suddenly started and looked around. "Where is Norma?" she asked; "Jugurtha, what have you done with my little one?" she added, almost fiercely, and pushing aside the cup she held in her lips.

"Hush, my mother!" he said, soothingly, "Norma is safe; God has taken care of her as well as of you and me."

"Then let me see her. Why doesn't she come to see me?" she asked, impatiently.

Jugurtha looked round to his master. "Could the child be brought here?" he asked.

The centurion looked perplexed. All the streets were so crowded with litters and foot passengers, that there was considerable difficulty in moving along, and for a child it would be dangerous to attempt such a passage, for everyone was eagerly pressing forward to catch a glimpse of the British princess Claudia, on her way to the villa, that had been prepared for her on the bank of the river.

At length he said, "I will try to bring her by and by;" and stepping forward he kindly and courteously asked after the prisoner's health.

But in a moment the haughty pride came back to her face as she recognized the dress of a Roman centurion.

"Leave us in peace," she said, in a commanding tone. "My son—" but there she stopped and glanced at Jugurtha's dress,—he was a slave, and she remembered the bitter fact now.

"Jugurtha, you said there was a good God somewhere. Where is He?" she asked.

"Here, Mother, in this very room," said Jugurtha.

The invalid looked round. "Where?" she asked, in a whisper. "I cannot see Him."

"No, Mother, we cannot see Him until we die, and go to the bright home He is getting ready for us beyond the clouds and stars,—a home where there are no slaves," he added, in a whisper; for slavery was very bitter to him, although he had so kind a master.

"No slaves," repeated Guntra. "Then could not this God set you free now?" she asked.

Jugurtha shook his head sadly. It seemed hopeless to expect or even to pray for such a thing. But to soothe his mother was his first thought now, and so he said,—

"As soon as you can move, you are to go where Norma is—where everyone will be kind to you, and you will learn to know this God of love."

"And you, my son, will you go with me?" asked Guntra, quickly.

Jugurtha looked down sadly, vainly trying to hide his emotion.

"I must stay here," he said.

He could not tell her she was in prison, and he must take her place. But his mother caught the sadness in his tone.

"You must stay here," she said. "Then I will stay too, for of what value is freedom to me if my son is a slave? But this God you talked about—you say He is good and kind, and has no slaves beyond the clouds. Could you not ask Him to make you free? Even our forest spirits will grant what is asked of them sometimes," she added.

Jugurtha looked round in perplexity, hoping to catch some intimation from his master of what answer he should give, but the centurion was gone.

"The great God does hear what men say to Him," answered Jugurtha, slowly; "but I never heard of any asking to be set free from the bonds of Roman slavery."

"Then you ask Him now," said Guntra, boldly and fearlessly. "If He is here, let the sacrifice be offered, and ask Him now."

"The sacrifice has been offered," said Jugurtha. "God sent His own Son to be the sacrifice, for He alone could bear our sins, and He bore them, and opened the way for us to ask God anything at any time."

INTIMATION: *hint*

"Then ask Him now to free us, Jugurtha—to free us and let us go back to our woods and people; ask Him to free our Britain too, and we will tell to our people the wonderful news that there is a God kind instead of cruel."

But Jugurtha still looked perplexed. His mother knew nothing of this God as yet, and of course thought of Him only as she did of the forest spirits, from whom some material benefits could be obtained; whereas Marcinius had taught him that it was spiritual blessings that should be sought from the Lord God Almighty. But as he thought thus, he repeated the name aloud, "Almighty! What does it mean if it is not this, that our God is great as well as good, all-powerful as well as loving? Mother, I will pray to Him for our freedom," he said, with sudden energy; "and oh! if we could teach our people to believe in Him, so that He became the God of Britain; I think I could even thank Him that the Romans came to our land, since they brought this great knowledge with them."

As he spoke Jugurtha knelt down beside his mother, and prayed aloud for deliverance from Roman bonds and slavery. But not for this alone; for his mother and his country he prayed too, that they might be delivered from the chains of superstition and the bondage of Satan, and brought into the glorious liberty of the children of God.

This was the only liberty he had ever dared to hope for yet, for Marcinius had to be very cautious how he spoke to his Christian converts, lest he and they should be accused of breaking the laws of Rome, and so bring discredit upon the new faith they hoped to recommend by their lives of patience and love. It was therefore a bold step Jugurtha thought to take upon himself, to speak to God upon a matter he had never yet heard of anyone else doing; but if it were wrong, he thought surely God would forgive him, since He was a God of love. This was His chief charac- teristic in the mind of Jugurtha and his fellow- Christians, and under that he sheltered himself now.

As he looked at his mother he saw that large tears were rolling down her thin white face.

"Jugurtha," she said, "I would that I knew more of this God. I have ceased to fear our forest spirits, and I would fain go and tell my people of this God of love."

"It may be we shall go," said Jugurtha; but the tone in which he spoke showed that he had little hope of this himself.

"Yet your God will hear you," said the invalid; "and I will ask Him too, for I cannot live a slave," she added.

"Our God is love," whispered Jugurtha. "And now, my mother, you must try and sleep again," he added; "in a few hours Norma may be here, but as yet the streets are too crowded for her to pass through them safely."

Guntra did not ask the cause of this; she felt weary and exhausted with the exertion of having said so much, and a few minutes afterwards fell asleep.

It was more painful to Jugurtha to leave his mother now than ever it had been before, because hitherto she had not been conscious of her surroundings; but now, if she should wake while he was away, he feared the keeper might—nay, would, without doubt, let her know where she actually was,—might even behave roughly to her if he had recently left the wineskin.

But this could not be helped. Jugurtha must go home for a short time, for his master would require his services; and as soon as he saw that his mother was asleep he left her, and made his way into the street.

A crowd of Roman citizens were just as eager sightseers in this year of A.D. 67 as a London crowd at the present day; and Jugurtha found it no easy matter to push his way through the streets, although he towered above the heads of many in that swaying, noisy multitude. He felt strongly inclined to wish the Princess Claudia had chosen some other time to visit London, for he was anxious to reach the soldiers' quarter as quickly as he could, that he might get back to his mother; and so he pushed and elbowed his way through, with more vigour than gentleness. But when the temple of Diana was reached all further progress seemed impossible, for here the crowd was impassable, and pausing in his efforts to struggle through the mass, he heard someone speaking in a loud, commanding tone.

At first he thought it was one of the priests of the goddess, or an attendant of the temple, exhorting the crowd not to press too closely into the sacred precincts, or relating some fable in her honour; but presently he heard a name that almost made him hold his breath in eager excitement,—it was the name of Jesus. There, from the portico of the temple of Diana, the news of His wonderful love was being proclaimed in the ears of hundreds of eager listeners.

At first Jugurtha doubted the evidence of his own senses as to this fact; and so eager did he become to assure himself of its truth, that he mounted the pedestal of a statue of Jupiter, that he might see and hear more clearly all that was going forward.

He had not been mistaken. There, in front of him, stood the slight figure of a Roman freedman, telling the story of God's love for man, and how the Lord of life and glory had come to redeem the world from the curse of evil. Jugurtha clasped his hands and closed his eyes in momentary thanksgiving. It was the first time he had ever heard the gospel publicly proclaimed, but it gave him encouragement to hope that this blessing would be given to his native land.

He was not allowed to remain long, however, in his elevated position. Some of those standing near

PORTICO: *a covered entrance area or porch where the roof is supported by pillars*

looked horrified at seeing him on the pedestal of their great deity, and he was pulled down without ceremony, receiving sundry hard blows, as well as hard words, for his want of reverence.

But someone, pitying his condition, retorted sharply, "It is well for you Romans to talk of the islanders insulting our great Jupiter, when you stand listening to one who will overthrow all our gods if he can."

"Who—who talks of overthrowing Jupiter and our great goddess Diana?" asked two or three angry voices together.

"Who should it be but yon brawler, who has learned his vain babbling from one of those scornful Jews—one who is even an outcast from his own people for this very thing, and has appealed unto Cæsar? He calls himself an apostle, by name Paul, who hath even bewitched the Princess Claudia herself, men say, even as this vain fellow is now bewitching you."

"Who says we are bewitched?" demanded several in the crowd.

"No one needs to say it, 'tis easy enough to see," said the stranger scornfully—and he pointed towards the marble portico of the temple. "There is the proof," he added; "if you were not bewitched would you stand here like dumb mules, and let yonder vain fellow overturn the worship of all that has made Rome great and the Romans renowned?"

By this allusion to their greatness, the people's pride was flattered, and they readily gave ear to the rest of his speech, and soon a cry was raised,—

"Down with him! down with him! he is a traitor to Rome and her gods."

In a few minutes the cry was taken up by the crowd, and the speaker's voice was drowned in the clamour of contending tongues, some more bold than the rest declaring that the stranger had done no harm—had not insulted the popular deities, and therefore should have a hearing. But these few were quickly silenced by the voices of the opposite party, and very soon the whole multitude took up the cry, and shouted,—

"Down with him! down with the traitor!"

Jugurtha knew that the violence, once commenced, would not end in mere words, and so he had struggled near the temple while the war of words was commencing at the back, that he might have an opportunity of giving some help to the stranger if it were necessary. While he was still struggling to the front, someone touched him on the shoulder, and he saw himself face to face with the girl who had first given him information about his mother.

She looked terribly anxious as she drew aside the veil that partly concealed her face.

"Oh, Briton, stop him! save him!" she cried in a hoarse whisper; "the people are already beginning to murmur against him."

"Do you know him?" said Jugurtha.

"Yes, oh, yes! he is my brother; he, too, was a slave. The Princess Claudia has freed him, but he still belongs to her household. Oh, save him, and I will ask her any favour for you, for I too am in her service now."

Jugurtha could not stay to tell the girl it was for no hope of reward that he was making almost superhuman efforts to reach the marble portico, for already that dreadful shout had begun, and he knew there was not a moment to lose if he would save the speaker from the fury of the mob.

At last he reached his side just as he ceased speaking. "Yield yourself to me, and I will protect you; I, too, am a Christian," whispered Jugurtha, and before the stranger had recovered from his astonishment, or the crowd knew what he was going to do, he had pushed him down the steps, and by his own commanding height, attracting all eyes to himself, he took the stranger's place as though he, too, were going to speak. The idea of a slave lecturing them caused some diversion in the crowd, which was just what Jugurtha wished and expected, for while they were indulging in various jokes at his expense, their intended victim escaped, and it was not until he was beyond their reach that they became aware of the fact. Jugurtha left his place then, highly elated that his ruse had been successful.

RUSE: *trick, strategy*

CHAPTER XII

THE PRINCESS CLAUDIA

JUGURTHA did not reach home so easily as he had anticipated. The crowd had been cheated of their victim, and seemed disposed to wreak their vengeance upon him as the cause of it; and after he had descended the steps he was pulled and pushed about with considerable violence, and received several blows in his efforts to escape. These, however, he scarcely felt while struggling with his antagonists, but when at last he got beyond the crowd, and the excitement had somewhat abated, he began to feel weak and faint, and then saw for the first time that his clothes were stained with blood.

Fortunately, he had struggled on in the direction of the soldiers' quarter, and a few minutes brought him to his master's house; but before he could cross the *atrium* he was overcome with faintness from the loss of blood, and sank down on the pavement with a deep groan.

Marcinius, who had been anxiously expecting Jugurtha for some time, heard him fall, and was getting alarmed when he saw the condition he was in. This was rather increased the next minute, when a soldier came in to summon him to go and quell a disturbance that was raging near the temple of Diana. "It has all been caused by one of these barbarian slaves," added the man, without noticing the bleeding figure close by.

Marcinius was, of course, obliged to leave Jugurtha for his wife to bind up his wounds, while he went and called out his men, and led them to where the mob was still fiercely contending. The sight of a centurion and his company, not at all famous for either justice or mercy when an attack was about to be made, had the effect of lulling the storm of words and blows a little; seeing which, Marcinius commanded his men to halt, hoping that the sight of his legionaries would be enough to disperse the crowd. This gave him an opportunity of hearing what had caused the disturbance; and his astonishment, like Jugurtha's, was great indeed, to hear that for more than an hour some bold disciple of the apostle at Rome had stood on those marble steps of the temple, and proclaimed to the people the wonderful news of the coming of the Son of God to redeem the world.

"It would have been better to have heard him out," said one, in a complaining tone; "words break no bones, and if the news he brings is truth,

QUELL: *quiet*

by the helmet of Cæsar a better day must be dawning for the world."

"A better day is dawning for the world," said Marcinius, quietly but impressively. "I know not who this stranger is, but it is said he comes from Rome, where there is a notable prisoner, one Paul, a Jew, who is the great God's messenger, and I doubt not he has learned these things from his lips. I would that I too had heard him," he added, with a sigh.

The man stared; Roman centurions were more given to boasting than anything else, and he could not understand Marcinius at all. At length he said,—

"Have you heard aught of this teaching before?"

Marcinius nodded.

"All men will hear of it now, I doubt not, since the Princess Claudia hath declared herself a Christian," he said.

"A Christian! What, one of the new sect that hath sprung up in Judea?" exclaimed the man.

"Yes; and I doubt not the stranger you heard here today was a Christian," replied Marcinius.

"Well, if it be so, I hope we shall hear more of their teaching here in Londinium," said the man.

Marcinius could not stay longer where he was. The crowd was breaking up in one part, only to re-collect and become more noisy in another, and so it became his duty to lead his men to this spot. By judicious management, however, the people were at last dispersed without a blow being struck

JUDICIOUS: *wise, careful*

on either side—a bloodless victory, of which Marcinius felt more proud than of any triumph he had
gained over the Britons.

When he returned home he found Jugurtha
better, but still weak from loss of blood, and likely
to make himself worse by his anxiety to return
to his mother. Such a thing was impossible now,
and Marcinius said so; but how Guntra was to be
otherwise attended he did not know. He heartily
wished his slave had made good his escape without any ill-usage; for the affair would get talked
about more now, and would probably come to the
Prætor's ears, who already felt himself deeply offended that his national duties had been so slight-
ed by the princess and her husband. He could not
blame Jugurtha for rescuing the preacher from the
fury of the mob, but the unpleasant consequences
likely to follow made him wish it were anyone else
than Jugurtha.

He was still pondering over the dilemma, when
the frightened face of a girl was seen peeping in
at the door. The centurion recognized her as the
one who had so often crept in when they met for
prayer, and he went forward to speak to her.

"What is it?" he said; "do you come with a message from the Prætor?"

"No, no; I am in the service of the Princess Claudia now," she replied. "But tell me, is he safe? my
brother feared he would be killed by that awful
mob."

"Who?" asked the centurion.

"Your slave, the Briton. He saved my brother's life, and my mistress is anxious to know whether he was hurt."

"Yes, he is hurt, but not killed," replied Marcinius; "although the blows he has received may be his death, unless his anxiety can be relieved concerning his mother."

"His mother? oh, I had forgotten her—the captive whom Master sent to the prison. Is she there still?" asked the girl.

"Yes, she is still very ill, and will be growing anxious that her son does not return; for he was on his way from the prison when he was stopped by the crowd round the temple. Will you go to her on your way back, and tell her that her son will return to her shortly, but cannot do so at once?"

"Yes, I will do anything I can for her," answered the girl, "for her son saved my brother;" and she readily agreed to take with her some more nourishment that had been prepared for the invalid.

On her way to the prison she formed a plan in her own mind to interest her new mistress in these two British captives. She had not been long with Claudia, but she had seen enough to know that works of love and charity were what her mistress specially delighted in; and she judged truly enough that the lady would be glad of an opportunity of showing kindness to her own countrymen, and that Guntra, as a woman, would have a special claim upon her.

So she did not stay long at the prison, but after attending to the invalid's immediate wants, hurried home to be in time to prepare her mistress for the bath, when she would have an opportunity of telling her all she had discovered concerning her brother's deliverer.

The lady was greatly concerned when she heard how seriously he had been wounded, and of his mother's dangerous state.

"I will myself go to see her tomorrow," she said, "and if possible bring her here until she recovers. What is the sum asked for her? do you know?" she added.

"Two hundred sesterces," replied the waiting-maid; and as she went on with her work of brushing her mistress' fair shining hair, she told her of Guntra being brought to the Prætor's house, wounded in the last battle between her countrymen and the Roman legions, and how she had refused to learn the duties of a waiting-maid.

The lady's cheek flushed angrily at the indignity that had been put upon her. If, as she believed she must be, this captive was chief of a tribe, she had a right, as a prisoner of the State, to better treatment than had been accorded her; and she resolved that justice should be done now.

"It is a disgrace to the Roman arms and the soldiers of the Emperor that a noble woman should be treated thus," she said, in a tone of anger.

"Yes, the Romans ever pride themselves on their clemency to those they conquer; but we see

CLEMENCY: *mercy*

little of it here," replied the girl.

Claudia did not answer. Personally she had much to thank the conquerors for; but she began to see that if favour was shown to one, cruelty was dealt out to hundreds, and that the boasted civilization of Rome had failed to make her people more kind or considerate than her own fierce, warlike, half-savage countrymen. She had learned, however, the great secret of all true refinement, the source of all true civilization, and she hoped and prayed that this gospel she had learned from the lips of the prisoner Paul, might yet refine and purify both Rome and Britain, and she resolved to make her first effort in teaching these truths with the captive she intended to release.

The following morning her litter was ordered early, and before the keeper of the prison had returned from his accustomed visit to the wine-shop close by, Claudia, attended by her maid, and one or two freedmen who walked beside her as an escort, were standing at the door.

The man was somewhat alarmed when summoned to attend the lady, but Claudia was not disposed to copy the overbearing manners of a Roman matron, and his fear subsided until he heard whom the lady wished to see, when he fairly shivered with terror and apprehension.

"I want to purchase this poor woman; the price asked is two hundred sesterces, I think," said Claudia, taking out a silken purse from the pouch at her girdle.

GIRDLE: *belt*

"You want her for a slave," uttered the man. "I was afraid she was your sister, lady, and you might be hard on a poor keeper."

Claudia smiled at the comical look of relief that spread itself over the man's face, but when she followed him into the little low-arched chamber where Guntra lay asleep, she did not wonder nor did she feel offended at the mistake he had made.

In spite of the change sickness had wrought in her, Guntra still looked regal and majestic, even as she lay on the rude bed of a slave; and Claudia, as she looked at her, did not wonder at her refusal to learn the duties of a waiting-maid.

"It is cruel, unjust," she said aloud, "and I will myself tell the Prætor I think so." Then turning to the keeper and one of her own servants who had followed her, she said, "Lift her gently and bear her to the litter ere she wakes;" then paying the man the price asked, and a trifle over for himself, she followed and was soon seated beside Guntra in the litter.

The movement had awakened her, but the sight of the waiting-maid, whom she recognized at once, dispelled her fears; and when she heard that she was to be taken to the house of the Princess Claudia she was quite content. But just as the lady was about to enter the litter a sudden thought of her children rushed across her mind, and she would have sprung out again but for the overpowering weakness.

"Let me go back," she cried, "I cannot come with you. It is a prison, I know, but my children can come to me there.—O Norma, Norma, I shall never see you now!"

"Hush! hush! you shall see your children if you wish it," said Claudia, soothingly. "I will send for your son as soon as we get home; be calm now, and I will take good care of you."

There was a look of wildness in Guntra's eyes as she turned and gazed at Claudia, but she no longer attempted to get out of the litter; and when the lady had seated herself by her side, she said slowly, "Did the great God send you to me? are you one of His servants?"

Claudia started. "Yes," she answered, scarcely knowing what else she could say.

"Then you know Him—this God of love Jugurtha has told me about. Will you teach me to know Him too? for He is good and kind, and listens when mortals ask a favour."

It was all Guntra knew of the "great God," but she believed in Him, and listened eagerly while Claudia told her more. The lady could scarcely speak for astonishment when she heard that this knowledge of the true God had preceded her to her native land, and she was more anxious than ever to see Jugurtha, and hear how this could be.

As soon as she reached home a litter was therefore sent to convey him and his sister to the elegant Roman villa where the princess had taken

up her residence. He was still weak and ill from
the wounds he had received the day before, but
he obeyed the command most joyfully when he
heard that his mother had already been removed
there; and it was an added pleasure that he could
at last restore his little sister to her arms.

When the excitement of meeting with her children had somewhat exhausted Guntra, Claudia
sent for them to her own apartment, and was surprised to find how much little Norma knew of the
life and teaching of the Lord Jesus, and how fully
and simply the child relied upon Him for everything.

"I asked Him not to take Jugurtha away from
me, but to bring Mother to us, and she's come;
but I don't think she likes London, so I have asked
God to take us all home again, that we may tell
the people in our village about Him," said Norma,
and it was said as though she had no doubt about
the answer.

"Where did you learn this?" asked the lady.

"Marcinius taught me," replied the little girl,
"and he heard it from one who knew the Lord Jesus, and went about with Him when He lived on
earth."

"Who is this Marcinius?" asked Claudia, turning
to Jugurtha, who stood at a respectful distance.

The young Briton bowed as he replied,—

"A Roman centurion—my master—who saved
us both from perishing in the woods when we

THE CHILD RESTORED

escaped from the Druid's knife; and he has taught us to fear neither Druid nor forest spirit, and we have learned to love the God of the Christians."

The answer, so simple and straightforward, pleased the lady, and she said,—

"You saved the life of one of my household yesterday, what can I do for you to show my gratitude for the service?"

For a moment Jugurtha's pale cheek flushed, and his heart beat quickly.

"Give me my freedom, and let me return to my own people," he was about to say; but he remembered his mother, and that she was a slave, and casting his eyes on the ground, he replied, "I ask no reward for helping a fellow-Christian, but if you will ransom my mother, and let her depart to her people, I will faithfully repay you all she may cost in money—the kindness can never be repaid."

Claudia felt proud of the native independence of her young countryman, slave though he was. She read too in his kindling eye, that had momentarily flashed with joy, how his own wish for freedom had been subdued for the sake of his mother, and she resolved to free both mother and children if she could. This resolve, however, she did not mention yet. Her husband must be consulted first upon the matter; and so telling the brother and sister they had better remain with their mother for a few days, she dismissed them.

CHAPTER XIII

CONCLUSION

SUMMER sunshine had again awakened all the beauties of wood and forest, and likewise added to the charms of the Roman gardens that skirted the banks of the winding Thames near Londinium. In one of the most beautiful of these, amidst delicate-looking dark-leaved ilexes and flowering myrtles, Jugurtha was walking with his mother, while little Norma ran round the various statues and urn-shaped vases with which the garden was studded.

Guntra still wore the long white robe that had distinguished her when in her native village, but Jugurtha had adopted a more becoming costume than the dirty sheepskin in which we first saw him. He was free now, so he no longer wore the dress of a slave, but out of gratitude to his benefactors, Claudia and Pudens, had adopted the Roman toga, and wore it gracefully too.

He looked more quiet and subdued, but withal far more happy than he had done twelve months before, when hunting the wild boar in his native forests. It was of these and the half-savage village he was thinking now, rather than the luxuriant garden in which he was walking.

"My mother, the Prætor is expected here tomorrow," said Jugurtha at length, after walking several times up and down the shady alley in silence.

Guntra started, and a faint colour came into her still pale face. She had recovered from her sickness, but was not very strong yet, and she dreaded to meet her captor.

"Jugurtha," she said, "I would this meeting could be spared me, for in my pride and haughtiness I spoke words unseemly the last time I saw this man. I knew not then what I know now, and I wonder not that he dealt harshly with me."

"But, my mother, whatever you said did not justify him in—"

"Nay, nay, he will not talk of this matter again, but what I did to cause it. My son, I was proud and imperious,—we Britons are ever so, and it will be hard for us to be Christians, hard for us to humble ourselves as this gospel teaches us we must."

"I know it," said Jugurtha, in a gentle tone, "and yet, oh, my mother, what do we not owe already to this gospel—this message of the God of love! If it had not been that Marcinius was a Christian we might never have met each other again, and now through this same constraining power of divine

UNSEEMLY: *inappropriate*
CONSTRAINING: *restraining*

love the noble Claudia is trying to restore us to our own people."

"Whether we are so restored or not, I am learning one thing, my son," said Guntra.

"Yes," replied Jugurtha, "your faith in the forest spirits was broken before you came to London, and so you were prepared to believe in the one true God and the Lord Jesus Christ, when you heard of Their love to mankind."

"But it is not all I have learned," said Guntra. "This gospel has taught me that the pride of our hearts must be subdued, and before I am baptized I will acknowledge my error to the Prætor, whether he allows me to depart from here or not."

Jugurtha looked surprised. His proud, haughty mother willing to acknowledge a fault—to an enemy, too,—it was something startling indeed. He knew nothing of the battle she had had over this matter, but he knew it must have cost her a severe struggle, from what he himself had endured in subduing this pride of heart in its various manifestations in himself.

"My mother," he said after a pause, "has the noble Claudia asked you to do this—to speak thus to the Prætor?"

"No, my son. I have told her of it—for it were mean to blame even an enemy more than is just,—but she said not aught of my acknowledging this fault."

"And you think you can speak humbly to this man, my mother?" said the young Briton, doubtfully.

"Our God will help me, Jugurtha," she said, in a gentle voice. "I am glad the ceremony of our baptism is not to take place until after the Prætor's visit here."

Jugurtha did not reply, for he was thinking that he had made a less noble confession of faith than his mother intended, although he had known this God of love so much longer. He too, with his little sister, was to be admitted as a member of the Christian church at the same time as his mother, and then he hoped the way would be opened for them to return to their native village. He would brave the fury of the Druids himself without fear, but he could not help feeling anxious sometimes concerning Norma. The dread of these priests and lawgivers of the land, seemed to have passed so entirely from his mother's mind, that she had not once expressed any fear of taking the child back, and only thought of the difficulties in the way from the Romans refusing to allow them to leave Londinium.

This, however, would soon be settled now. Pudens had used all his influence as a Roman general, both with the Prætor and Prefect; and it was hoped that when they came the following day they would give their consent for the three to leave Londinium at once.

No one but Jugurtha was aware of what his mother intended doing when the Prætor came, and therefore Claudia was not a little surprised to see Guntra take the position of a slave when the Prætor entered the *atrium* the next day. Not as a slave, but as an honoured guest, was she treated now by the Princess Claudia, who was therefore greatly astonished at seeing her take this humble position.

In a few minutes, however, it was explained. Guntra acknowledged in the presence of all, the fault of which she had been guilty, the ingratitude of it after the kind treatment she had received from the Prætor; and then declared it was the teaching of the gospel that had taught her to see that this was wrong.

Everyone was astonished, and none more so than the Prætor himself. "Truly there must be some wondrous power in this new faith," he said. "I did not think it was possible for anything to subdue so proud a spirit as this woman's, but your Christianity has subdued and yet ennobled her."

The proud Roman, in his astonishment, forgot his state, and that Guntra had once been a slave in his household, and taking her by the hand he gently led her to a tent near her young hostess, begging her at the same time to think no more of what had passed, and to remember only her captivity by the kind friends she had gained through it; and he looked at Claudia as he spoke.

That Guntra had by this gained the goodwill of the Prætor was evident to all; the Princess Claudia was therefore greatly surprised and not a little disappointed when she heard that the only terms upon which he would let his British captives return home was that Guntra should swear allegiance to the Emperor, and leave her daughter in one of the Roman camps, as a hostage, for one year.

Bitter indeed were such terms to Guntra, and at first she positively refused to accept them, but Jugurtha saw in them the solving of a great difficulty.

"My mother, cannot you believe that 'God is love' even in this?" he said. "It is hard, very hard to leave our Norma for a year, even with such a kind friend as the noble Claudia, who has promised to be her guardian. But would it not be harder to know that she fell a victim to the Druid's knife and fire? My mother, you forget the old superstition, and the danger from which I rescued the little one."

Guntra started and turned pale. "True, true, I *did* forget," she said; "and you too, Jugurtha, will be in danger."

"Do not fear for me, my mother, the Druids shall not harm me; but we could not always be watching Norma, neither could we make her understand the danger she was in; but changes may come in the course of a year. I hope many of our people will learn to cast off the old superstition, and that with our sworn allegiance to Rome will be a protection to the little one."

Jugurtha continued to talk cheeringly and hopefully, but his mother still looked anxious and distressed at the thought of leaving little Norma, even with such a kind friend as the Princess Claudia.

But she could not long indulge her despondency. Preparations were already being made for her departure with Jugurtha, and one or two of their warriors redeemed from slavery by the kindness of Claudia and Pudens, and immediately after their baptism they would leave Londinium under an escort commanded by their old friend Marcinius. He had been chosen for this difficult task, because of his judicious management of the mob on the day of the disturbance near the temple, for it was thought there might be some difficulty with the Britons receiving their chief again, more especially when it became known that she had sworn allegiance to the Romans.

But before setting out on this diplomatic mission, Marcinius had one more friendly task to perform for Jugurtha. As his friend and instructor in the faith of Christ it became his duty to lead him to the water's edge when he should be baptized. It was a solemn and yet a joyful meeting that took place at Claudia's house on this occasion.

An old man, who like the princess had learned the truth from the lips of the apostle, engaged in prayer, and then after an exhortation led the way through the garden to the bank of the river. Guntra, led by the Princess Claudia, was the first baptized, and then Norma, led by the same lady. Afterwards came Jugurtha, led by the Roman centurion, and then the rest of the converts, some of whom were going back with their chief to spread the knowledge of the truth among their countrymen. Each was baptized in the name of the Father, the Son, and the Holy Ghost—firstfruits to God of the harvest that should be reaped from the barbarian land of Britain. The young princess was almost overcome with joy and thankfulness. She had come with high hopes and sanguine expectations from Rome, but these had been far exceeded, for she found that the seed of the kingdom had already been sown, and was bearing fruit in the lives of more than one of her countrymen.

The day following that on which they were baptized, the British captives departed from London, many of them with tears of regret for the kind friends left behind, but none more sorrowful than Guntra and Jugurtha. The British matron had formed a strong attachment to the Princess Claudia, from whom she had learned so much concerning the Christian faith, but harder than leaving her, was it to leave little Norma behind. Jugurtha grieved too for his little sister, and yet he could not but feel thankful that she was not

SANGUINE: *confident*

coming with them, for she might speedily fall a victim to the cruelty of the Druids, whose power over the minds of his countrymen it was his full determination to endeavour to break.

The march with their Roman escort was necessarily slow and tedious, but at length they came within sight of their native village, and Guntra standing up in her war chariot—which had been presented to her by the Prætor just before leaving —could see that the men were hurrying to and fro, bringing out spears and their skin-covered targets to resist the expected attack of the Romans.

She sent at once for Marcinius. "Stop your people," she cried, "and let me and my son go forward, that my warriors may see we come as friends, not foes,—that the Romans can bring peace as well as war."

The centurion hesitated for a moment. He could see now that the Britons were preparing to fight, and if a blow was once struck on either side, there was no telling where it would end, and yet he dared not allow Guntra to go alone to the village, for fear her countrymen should refuse to receive her. So he called out ten of his oldest veterans, and commanding the others to halt, he went forward with them as a guard of honour to Guntra and Jugurtha.

The sight of a British war chariot and the white-robed figure of a woman seemed to fill the Britons with amazement, and not only men but women

THE RETURN HOME

and children very soon ventured beyond the palisades of the village. In a few minutes Guntra was recognized, and then with a loud shout of welcome the people ran forward to meet her.

Marcinius understood the shout, and he and his men paused while the British captives went forward to meet their friends. There was little fear of the villagers not receiving them; and the only power now to dread was the Druids. But after some conversation held with the chief men of her tribe, Guntra found that they had interfered very little with the people lately. The signal failure of all their predictions, and the disastrous termination of the attack on the Romans on which they had been sent, had greatly tended to break the faith of the people both in their gods and teachers; and when Guntra told them that she and her son had been protected and cared for by another God, whom they had now vowed to serve and worship, the Britons made no objection. They had not chosen another chief, for faint rumours had reached them that neither Guntra nor Jugurtha were dead, and they knew if it were possible she would return, and so they had agreed to wait one year at least for her coming.

There was only one thing in the way of the peaceful settlement of the whole question, and that was the alliance with the Romans. The spirit of the proud Britons chafed against swearing allegiance to Rome; but when at last they

SIGNAL: *notable*

understood it was the only condition upon which
Guntra and Jugurtha could be allowed to remain,
they resolved to ratify what their chief had already
done.

They were somewhat puzzled at the affection-
ate parting between the Roman centurion and
their young chief, for Marcinius had learned to
love Jugurtha as a son, while he looked upon the
Roman soldier as his dearest earthly friend—his
father in Christ Jesus. It was, therefore, no easy
matter for him to part with Marcinius; and long
and earnest was the talk between the two before
the centurion led his soldiers back towards Londinium.

Of course, having formed an alliance with
Rome, there would be little for the warriors of the
tribe to do now,—a state of things Jugurtha had
foreseen, and provided against. He himself had
learned many of the arts of civilization during
his stay in the Roman camp, and these he at once
began to teach his fellow-countrymen, while his
mother did much to help the women prepare better food and clothing for themselves and families.

But these arts of peace were not all Guntra and
Jugurtha taught to their people. The young Briton
had learned to read, and from a scroll, presented
to him by the Princess Claudia, he read the story
of the life and death of the God-man Christ Jesus;
and that picture of redeeming love soon penetrat-
ed the hearts of men and women who had scarcely

RATIFY: *confirm*

ever wept before, but now shed tears as they heard of the wondrous love of God.

Before the time came for Norma to be delivered up by the Romans, the whole village professed Christianity, and most of them were humble and consistent followers of Christ. There was, therefore, no fear that the little girl would be given up as a victim to the old superstition; but when she came back the whole village rejoiced, and thanked God for the return of the last of those through whose captivity such great blessings had been sent to them.

THE END

ABOUT THE AUTHOR

Emma Leslie (1837-1909), whose actual name was Emma Dixon, lived in Lewisham, Kent, in the south of England. She was a prolific Victorian children's author who wrote over 100 books. Emma Leslie's first book, *The Two Orphans*, was published in 1863 and her books remained in print for years after her death. She is buried at the St. Mary's Parish Church, in Pwllcrochan, Pembroke, South Wales.

Emma Leslie brought a strong Christian emphasis into her writing and many of her books were published by the Religious Tract Society. Her extensive historical fiction works covered many important periods in church history. Her writing also included a short booklet on the life of Queen Victoria published in the 50th year of the Queen's reign.

Emma Leslie Church History Series

GLAUCIA THE GREEK SLAVE
A Tale of Athens in the First Century
After the death of her father, Glaucia is sold to a wealthy Roman family to pay his debts. She tries hard to adjust to her new life but longs to find a God who can love even a slave. Meanwhile, her brother, Laon, struggles to find her and to earn enough money to buy her freedom. But what is the mystery that surrounds their mother's disappearance years earlier and will they ever be able to read the message in the parchments she left for them?

OUT OF THE MOUTH OF THE LION
Or, The Church in the Catacombs
When Flaminius, a high Roman official, takes his wife, Flavia, to the Colosseum to see Christians thrown to the lions, he has no idea the effect it will have. Flavia cannot forget the faith of the martyrs, and finally, to protect her from complete disgrace or even danger, Flaminius requests a transfer to a more remote government post. As he and his family travel to the seven cities of Asia Minor mentioned in Revelation, he sees the various responses of the churches to persecution. His attitude toward the despised Christians begins to change, but does he dare forsake the gods of Rome and embrace the Lord Jesus Christ?

SOWING BESIDE ALL WATERS
A Tale of the World in the Church
There is newfound freedom from persecution for Christians under the emperor, Constantine, but newfound troubles as well. Errors and pagan ways are creeping into the Church, while many of the most devoted Christians are withdrawing from the world into the desert as hermits and nuns. Quadratus, one of the emperor's special guards, is concerned over these developments, even in his own family. Then a riot sweeps through the city and Quadratus' home is ransacked. When he regains consciousness, he finds that his sister, Placidia, is gone. Where is she? And can the Church handle the new freedom, and remain faithful?

www.SalemRidgePress.com

EMMA LESLIE CHURCH HISTORY SERIES

FROM BONDAGE TO FREEDOM
A Tale of the Times of Mohammed
At a Syrian market two Christian women are sold as slaves. One of the slaves ends up in Rome where Bishop Gregory is teaching his new doctrine of "purgatory" and the need for Christians to finish paying for their own sins. The other slave travels with her new master, Mohammed, back to Arabia, where Mohammed eventually declares himself to be the prophet of God. In Rome and Arabia, the two women and countless others fall into the bondage of man-made religions—will they learn at last to find true freedom in the Lord Jesus Christ alone?

THE MARTYR'S VICTORY
A Story of Danish England
Knowing full well they may die in the attempt, a small band of monks sets out to convert the savage Danes who have laid waste to the surrounding countryside year after year. The monks' faith is sorely tested as they face opposition from the angry Priest of Odin as well as doubts, sickness and starvation, but their leader, Osric, is unwavering in his attempts to share the "White Christ" with those who reject Him. Then the monks discover a young Christian woman who has escaped being sacrificed to the Danish gods—can she help reach those who had enslaved her and tried to kill her?

GYTHA'S MESSAGE
A Tale of Saxon England
Having discovered God's love for her, Gytha, a young slave, longs to escape the violence and cruelty of the world and devote herself to learning more about this God of love. Instead she lives in a Saxon household that despises the name of Christ. Her simple faith and devoted service bring hope and purpose to those around her, especially during the dark days when England is defeated by William the Conqueror. Through all of her trials, can Gytha learn to trust that God often has greater work for us to do *in* the world than *out* of it?

www.SalemRidgePress.com

Additional Titles Available From

Salem Ridge Press

YUSSUF THE GUIDE
Being the Strange Story of the Travels in Asia Minor of
Burne the Lawyer, Preston the Professor, and
Lawrence the Sick
by George Manville Fenn
Illustrated by John Schönberg

Young Lawrence, an invalid, convinces his guardians, Preston the Professor and Burne the Lawyer, to take him along on an archaeological expedition to Turkey. Before they set out, they engage Yussuf as their guide. Through the months that follow, the friends travel deeper and deeper into the remote regions of central Turkey on their trusty horses in search of ancient ruins. Yussuf proves his worth time and time again as they face dangers from a murderous ship captain, poisonous snakes, sheer precipices, bands of robbers and more. Memorable characters, humor and adventure abound in this exciting story!

MARIE'S HOME
Or, A Glimpse of the Past
by Caroline Austin
Illustrated by Gordon Browne R. I.

Eleven-year-old Marie Hamilton and her family travel to France at the invitation of Louis XVI, just before the start of the French Revolution. There they encounter the tremendous disparity between the proud French Nobility and the oppressed and starving French people. When an enraged mob storms the palace of Versailles, Marie and her family are rescued from grave danger by a strange twist of events, but Marie's story of courage, self-sacrifice and true nobility is not yet over! Honor, duty, compassion and forgiveness are all portrayed in this uplifting story.

www.SalemRidgePress.com

For Younger Readers

DOWN THE SNOW STAIRS
Or, From Goodnight to Goodmorning
by Alice Corkran
Illustrated by Gordon Browne R. I.

On Christmas Eve, eight-year-old Kitty cannot sleep, knowing that her beloved little brother is critically ill due to her own
disobedience. Traveling in a dream to Naughty Children Land,
she meets many strange people, including Daddy Coax and Lady
Love. Kitty longs to return to the Path of Obedience but can she
resist the many temptations she faces? Will she find her way home
in time for Christmas? An imaginative and delightful read-aloud
for the whole family!

SOLDIER FRITZ
A Story of the Reformation
by Emma Leslie
Illustrated by C. A. Ferrier

Young Fritz wants to follow in the footsteps of Martin Luther
and be a soldier for the Lord, so he chooses a Bible from the
peddler's pack as his birthday gift. When his father, the Count,
goes off to war, however, Fritz and his mother and little sister are
forced to flee into the forest to escape being thrown in prison
for their new faith. Disguising themselves as commoners, they
must trust the Lord as they wait and hope for the Count to rescue
them. But how will he ever be able to find them?

AMERICAN TWINS OF THE REVOLUTION
Written and illustrated by Lucy Fitch Perkins

General Washington has no money to pay his discouraged
troops and twins Sally and Roger are asked by their father,
General Priestly, to help hide a shipment of gold which will be
used to pay the American soldiers. Unfortunately, British spies
have also learned about the gold and will stop at nothing to
prevent it from reaching General Washington. Based on a true
story, this is a thrilling episode from our nation's history!

www.SalemRidgePress.com

Historical Fiction by William W. Canfield

THE WHITE SENECA
Illustrated by G. A. Harker
Captured by the Senecas, fifteen-year-old Henry Cochrane grows to love the Indian ways and becomes Dundiswa—the White Seneca. When Henry is captured by an enemy tribe, however, he must make a desperate attempt to escape from them and rescue fellow captive, Constance Leonard. He will need all the skills he has learned from the Indians, as well as great courage and determination, if he is to succeed. But what will happen to the young woman if they do reach safety? And will he ever be able to return to his own people?

AT SENECA CASTLE
Illustrated by G. A. Harker
In this sequel to *The White Seneca*, Henry Cochrane, now eighteen, faces many perils as he serves as a scout for the Continental Army. General Washington is determined to do whatever it takes to stop the constant Indian attacks on the settlers and yet Henry is torn between his love for the Senecas and his loyalty to his own people. As the Army advances across New York State, Henry receives permission to travel ahead and warn his Indian friends of the coming destruction. But will he reach them in time? And what has happened to the beautiful Constance Leonard whom he had been forced to leave in captivity a year earlier?

THE SIGN ABOVE THE DOOR
Young Prince Martiesen is ruler of the land of Goshen in Egypt, where the Hebrews live. Eight plagues have already come upon Egypt and now Martiesen has been forced by Pharaoh to further increase the burden of the Hebrews. Martiesen, however, is in love with the beautiful Hebrew maiden, Elisheba, whom he is forbidden by Egyptian law to marry. As the nation despairs, the other nobles turn to Martiesen for leadership, but before he can decide what to do, Elisheba is kidnapped by the evil Peshala and terrifying darkness falls over the land. An exciting tale woven around the events of the Exodus from the Egyptian perspective!

www.SalemRidgePress.com

CPSIA information can be obtained at www.ICGtesting.com
Printed in the USA
LVOW051257181212

312177LV00001B/24/A